KB070719

그리움
한
두레박

An empty bucket evokes saudade

白山 南伯鉉

희망의 서문

숨 푸른 향나무에 기대어
그리움으로 빈 두레박

김매기에 허리 쭉 해거름
엄마 손의 오싹한 등목을
뙤약볕 훔쳐 웃던 매미가
훨훨 날아버린 굴뚝 너머

마른 가지에 홍시 두 개
노을은 잔물져 애타는데

꿈을 겨루며 달린 분초랑
워워 쉼터에 닿은 허공이
돌아가고픈 날을 못 잊어
눈 말간 우물을 저어대면

아무래도
가슴 도근거리는 예 깊이
속 쌀뜨물 동그라니 서린
달빛을 떠야겠습니다

2022. 2. 2
백산 남 백 현

Preface to hope in my 70s

An empty bucket in search of saudade
Leaning on the vividly breathing juniper

The sun sets after weeding with a hard back
Mom washed my back chillingly
Cicada smiling while wiping the scorching sun
Over the chimney, it fluttered away

Two red persimmons hanging on a dry branch
The softly colored evening glow is painful

Time we competed for our dreams and
Whoa whoa, Space barely reached the shelter
Can't forget the days they missed
Stir up the clean well with hopeful eyes

Inevitably
I have to scoop up the noble moonlight
that the final rice water rises in a circle
in this deep place where my heart is pounding

2022. 2. 2
White mountain

목차

– 소망

- 자연치유

- 풍경

– In English

001. 라면 국물

빙 둘러앉아 한 젓가락 후루룩
침샘 고이듯 정이 쌓이고
밴 섬 내에 늙어간 향이 나도
추억같이 다시는 모두의 입맛

식탐하는 영감은 국물에 밥을 말고
알음직한 목발의 젊은이가
해롭다며 만류하는 염려에

보글보글 끓어 바라지 다한 국물은
얄궂은 무명 따라 입으로 싱크대로
굴레 벗어 흐르는데

내버리는 라면 국물은
자꾸 서글퍼지는 목을 타고
어스름 녘 요양원의
가녀려운 불빛을 흔든다

*무명(無明) : 마음, 마음의 상태

002. 억새꽃

열심히 살라시며
아이 맘을 다잡고
바랜 두루마기 흰 고무신에
노을 너머로 가신 할아버지

까투리 푸드덕 숨바꼭질하는
덤불 드문드문 억새 동산엔
뜰 듯 뜰 듯 부활의
먼 말발굽 소리

두고 간 억새꽃
마른 눈물이
별을 따오라
어둠을 열면

잘 가라
어서 가라
하얀 손을 흔들지만

돌아서는 깨금발에

가지 마라
가지 마라
억세게 여윈 혼
애처로이 나부낀다

003. 고려 요양장

토실 밤 주우러 산토끼는 떠나고
파랑새는 청포장술 굳이 울리네
복숭아 살구꽃 그리운 진달래
 꿈 피던 산골은 지고 없는데

엄마가 애타게 엄마를 찾아
시렁 위의 물레를 엘레지로 돌리고
돌리고 돌려도 허공의 물레에
 헛 저은 날들이 마냥 서럽고

할머니는 아버지를 가련히 불러
목쉬어 밤 쉬도록 애달파해도
등 돌려 바쁜 열 발가락 아이들
 하얀 그림자만 아스라하여

갠 이불 다시 접고
먹은 밥 또 찾아도
 배고픈 아침 마흔아홉 시

올 수도 갈 수도 엉킨 길 위에
손 놓은 하늘과 땅이
　혼돈으로 비빈 천국

흠뻑 땀도 미소로 닦던 달님이
한 겹 흙 고개를 차마 못 넘어
손사래 치고 넋을 접는 마당을
　불효가 숨어 찾는 고려 요양장

004. 우리 엄마

도르륵 재봉틀에 엄마 손이 닿으면
버선에 두루마기가 척척 나오고
알록달록 뜨개질에 따뜻한 내 장갑

삼십 리 장바구니 머리에 이고
땅기는 다리를 감춘 고무신이
신기루에 어리는 우리 엄마

성모님 사임당 황후나 퀴리 부인이
아무리 위대한들
우리 엄마 발아래요

은하수 별똥별 북두칠성 샛별이
모두 반짝여도
날 비추는 우리 엄마만 하랴

어긋난 아이 마다치 않으시고
숭고한 사랑의 약손으로
깨어나라 미소 짓는 엄마 얼굴

달 들고 물 긷는 그리움 끝에는
불멸의 포근한 가슴으로
한없이 자랑스러운 우리 엄마

패배에 수치의 위축도 다치지도 않게
묵묵히 마음을 단련하여
마지막에 웃어야 한다며
구멍 난 양말을 야무지게 꿰매주셨지

005. 설악의 밤

서러이 피고 진 부지런한 오계절
충충이 고인 이슬 아득한 쓰라림
저리고 멍든 마디마디 찬 오름에
골골이 무명 치마 숨죽인 금낭화

살아서는 죽어도 모를
가고 나면 뭉친 가슴 치며
지는 산 위로 애타게 앓아
노을 붉은 바다

달빛에 구름 타고 용틀임하는
한 떨기 조각 염원은
하늘가 막막 길을 물어 더듬고

거친 모두숨의 봉정 큰 바위는
마주 못 할 눈이 가로젓는 고개에
내일이면 가고 마는
잊은 오늘을 살라 하며
긴 금을 긋는 까마아득 별똥별

마른 굴뚝이 타는 가슴에
애절하게 포갠 두 손으로
목메어 두드린 설악의 밤

예외규정이 수두룩한 법 천지인데
천국령에 애이불비 한길 여시어
한 번만 다시 오시면
안 되겠습니까?
어머니!

006. 마지막 첫날

울어 삼백 일 비가 되고
열이렛날 보름달이 일그러져도
고개 들면 환한 금빛 얼굴이여

낭떠러지에 걸린 바람이
헐떡이는 숨 몰아 머문 곳에는
잘 아는 아이들의 목멘 눈동자

돌아올 길 모르는 출발선에서
내려놓은 모두는 타버린 불꽃

참매미 한 모금씩 사른 여름을
장마야 너도 흐느껴 아프구나

천사의 마중물 무지개다릴 딛고
엷은 미소 가물가물 흩날리는 구름에
여기의 마지막은 가는 그곳 첫날이라

외진 들판 푸른 설움에
뜸
뜸
뜸부기 운다

007. 목련에 앉은 까치

겨우내 잘 잔 목련은
하얀 깃을 반짝이며
까치가 속삭이는 간지럼에
첫사랑의 향기를
바다 넓은 두 팔로
기지개 켜나 보다

봉긋 여민 가슴속
풋풋한 초록 향기는
아지랑이 너울에 춤추는 나비

산새가 알 꼭 품은
꿈 젖어 처연한 무덤 너머로
엄마랑 다듬던 꽃밭을 거닐다가

청량한 목련의 함소에
저리고 엉킨 숨 한참을 풀치고

긴 하늘 훠이 휘돌아온 가지에
한숨보다 짧은 봄날은
하얗게 뭉치는데

안경 너머로 검은 비닐이 깍깍거리고
목련도 어제처럼 푸르지는 않나 보다

008. 그리움 한 두레박

마음 저은 낮달은 뽀얀 면사폴 벗어두고
누굴 보려 달린 해도 한 모금 목 축이려
긴 끈을 적시던 도란도란 우물가

미래로 과거로 모두 가고 남은 터에
짙은 꿈을 기대어 바람 담는 두레박
뭉친 날 궁금하여 바짝 귀 기울이니
차곡차곡 덮어둔 그리움만 조잘조잘

구정물로 삭힌 감에 멍든 능금이
그렇게도 맛있는 줄 몰랐던 시절
한가득한 숨으로 출렁인 두레박이
쏟아주는 목물로 혼비백산 무더위

후드득 소나기가 기다림으로 쏟아지면
굳은 땅은 가슴 풀어 물방구를 피우고
기단 너머 낙숫물에 추녀 깊은 옹당이
땅찌미를 주워 담던 시름 가득 소쿠리
허기진 날들이 석류알처럼 아물었어도

부지런히 내달린 한여름 땀 세월에
짧고도 긴긴날을 눌러 담은 기억이
애잔하게 맴도는 그리움 한 두레박

개울 뜬 소금쟁이 뭉게구름 누벼대고
서슬 퍼런 이파리 삼복을 나부끼는데
보고픔의 맨 끝에 두레박을 당기는
황금 면류관의 사무치는 우리 엄마

009. 푸른 잎의 유영

그리움 한 잎이
그렇게 싱싱한 여름날을 비웁니다

그늘로 초복을 위로해주던
그리도 잘생긴 푸르름이
그림자가 길어지기도 전에
그리움으로 하늘을 가립니다

남은 이파리는
비바람이 좋아라 나폴대건만
하얀 혼을 어찌 남기고
포도 위로 아스라이 멀어지나요

요만큼만 더 긴 숨이 뜨거웠어도
물씬 고운 단풍에
웃음 찍는 소리로 부풀 터인데
누가 그리 급하게 부르던가요

메마른 가지에 까마귀 두 마리
부리를 깍지 끼고 행복을 부비는데
푸른 잎은 한없이 푸르러야 했건만
그 맛을 알지도 못하고

어이 가셨나요
애절한 청춘이여
가기는 잘 가셨나요
막힌 가슴에 꾹꾹 처량비만 고입니다

010. 불두화

일었던 불꽃을 곰곰이 더듬어보면
무슨 꽃을 좋아하느냐고 물었을 때
어떤 꽃이라고 말할 수 없었던 것은
좋아할 만한 꽃이 없었기 때문이지요

어떤 꽃에 마음을 둘까 둘러보아도
그리 그런 즐거운 꽃들은 숨어 돌고
올망졸망 뽐내던 앙증맞은 채송화는
열흘이 흐른 시절 따라 가버렸다오

어느 날인가 앞마당 대추나무 가까이
눈꽃처럼 솜사탕처럼 초록 손을 펴고
늘 보던 그 자리에 하얀 미소 머금은
불동화 그윽한 송이가 일색이었지요

땅거미 섧게 사무치고 밤 깊어가는데
하얀 불똥을 흐드러지게 피우는 꿈은
창가에 멈칫하는 왕방울 같은 눈꽃이
보고픈 엄마의 애처로운 넋일 테지요

011. 사랑

사랑아 너는
누구를 사랑하느냐

사랑아 어찌
정을 두고 가려느냐

그 맑은 눈망울에
보름달을 흐려놓고
먼 산 넘어가는 씁쓸한 구름 치마

쏟아지는 그리움에
물거품은 부풀고
하나둘 초록 잎이 알록달록 잠들면
탱자나무 울타리 안에
홍시는 뜨거운데

불꽃처럼 사라지는 혼불이 아니기를
애타는 몸부림의 긴 기다림

그 끄트머리에
목놓아 걸어두고
이별 따라 줄달음치는 사랑

사랑아
네가 밉다

012. 다리 짚기 놀이

무명 치마에 찬바람 감추던 이월 초하루
장독대에 촛불 켜고 떡시루에 칼을 꽂고
간절한 두 손 모아 영두할마이 축원하여
우리 엄마 염원 애절하게 꽃피우던 날에

구들목에 동생과 마주 앉아
다리를 엇끼우고 가락 넣어
부푼 꿈을 다듬던 놀이

『이거리· 저거리· 각· 거리
 동서· 맹건· 두맹· 건
 추무리· 바꾸· 두바· 꾸
 연지· 탕개· 열두· 냥
 가· 상· 워· 리
 영· 두· 칼· 침· 폭』

손으로 다리를 차례로 짚어가며
스물다섯 장단 맞추어 흥얼거리다가
마지막 폭에 짚은 다리를 빼는데

두 다리가 먼저 빠지면 이기는 놀이에
시작 자리 바꾸어 동생이 이기게 하면
침울하던 아이는 신이 나고
져준 마음이 즐겁던 하루가
별꽃처럼 눈꽃처럼
마디마디 포개져 가물가물 시린 추억

*『이 거리 저 거리 각 거리 동서 맹건 두 맹건
　추무리 바꾸 두 바꾸 연지 탕개 열두 냥
　가상 월이 영두 칼침 폭』
　: 머리에 망건을 두르고 가발을 올리는 과정을 장단 맞추어 흥얼거리던 가락으로 다리 짚기
　　놀이하면서 재미있게 불렀던 가사
*동서 : 앞뒤 또는 좌우
*두 맹건 : 머리의 망건
*추무리 : 옹기그릇, 머리둘레
*바꾸 : 바퀴
*연지 : 종이 끈
*탕개 : 물건의 동인 줄을 죄는 물건
*가상 : 거짓 현상
*월이 : 딴 머리, 덧 머리
*가상 월이 : 달비, 가발
*영두 칼침 폭 : 음력 이월 초 영등제의 시루떡 판에 칼을 꽂듯이 달비를 얹어 고정하려고 비
　　　　　　　녀를 꽂는 동작의 표현

013. 허공

깨방치기하면서 손자와 놀다 보니
흐느적흐느적 둥근 벽시계
열아흐레 월광을 물끄러미 닮아 섧고

구슬치기 자치기에 아련한 총총걸음
풍개 앵두 우물가를 훨훨 나비더니
청춘도 바람도 잠든 두레박에
동지섣달 하얀 밤만 소복 쌓아두었네

가고 아니 오는 흔적 간절하건만
체념도 초월도 굳게 다물어
후두엽을 가린 벼랑 끝에서
한 움큼 잡초 든 손에
꾸역꾸역 두드린 허공

* 깨방치기: 귀여운 동물이나 아이를 못살게 굴 정도로 귀여워하며 노는 행동

014. 빈 화병

보라비단 받침에
초록 포 살그미 드리우고
봄 굴러 발그레 열여섯 수려한 잎

꿀 담은 두 술 차곡히
맵시 도드라진
한 송이 꽃을

꽃병에 꽂으려는데

아
그만
꿈이 깨어 버렸네

015. 나와 너의 사랑, 아리랑

나와 너의 사랑, 나와 너의 사랑, 내가 당신을 붙들 일이요
나와 너의 사랑이 고비를 넘고 있다네

『아리랑 아리랑 아라리요
　아리랑 고개를 넘어간다』

나와 너 나와 너의 사랑, 남과 너 남과 너의 사랑
내가 당신을 붙들 일이 생겼네
나와 너의 사랑의 고비에 날 넘도록 해주구려

『아리 아리랑 쓰리 쓰리랑
　아라리가 났네
　아리랑 고개로 날 넘겨주소』

나와 너 나와 너, 남과 너 남과 너
내가 당신을 붙들 일이요

『아리아리 쓰리쓰리
　아라리요』

옛날 옛적 우리 사랑 가슴 쓰린 고비여
나와 너의 사랑을 탐내고 있었네
우리 사이에 티끌이 없었다면 좋았으련

이다지 쓰린 날이 언제 지나가려나
주룩주룩 사무치는 십 리 먼 고비에
행주치마 찬바람은 세월만 나부끼네

나 없이는 못 살 당신이여
내 마음 부디 헤아리시어
떠나려 말고 어서 돌아오소서

016. 오래된 가을

초가지붕 둥실 박 덩굴 사이로
깍 깍 깍 꽁지를 까불면
사립문에 기댄 싸리비 들고
오랜 누구를 괜스레 기다려

터질 듯 탐스런 갈색 고욤은
막내 잠자리 뱌비대는 엄마의 품
알록달록 가지마다 여민 홍시에
길손은 먼 하늘 무지개 둥둥

대청마루에 솔바람 갸웃거리며
한 장 두 장 홀로 책장 넘길 때
물동이를 인 손목 뜨겁게 잡고
파르르 심었던 첫서리 언약

철철 두레박에 꾸벅꾸벅 반달도
하얀 도포 자락에 숨은 이야기도
흩어진 전설을 목말라 쓸면
솔가리로 가린 술독은 보그르르

도란도란 정 흐르는 도랑물 위로
단풍잎 노 저어 그리움 고적한 채
높맑은 햇살은 바지런히 여무는데

찰나의 푸르른 꿈
옛날에 서서
오래된 가을을 그려봅니다

017. 겨운 그리움

담기조차 아까워 셔터도 파르르 떤
아침 산길에 마주친
고운매 꽃 한 송이

머물고픈 마음 못내 추스르며
행여 다칠세라 풀숲 골라 에워두고

애태운 그 자리에 헐레벌떡
부푼 걸음으로 돌아오니
아뿔싸

댕강 줄기는 이차돈의 혼을 맺고
콩닥콩닥 피운 정이
물안개보다 허우룩한
연이 되어버렸네

곱씹어 맴도는 촉촉한 자락에
다시 움트는 염원도 설워
품어 겨운 그리움은
휑한 하늘가 한 서린 꽃 숨소리

018. 진달래 동산

아른아른 청람에 여린 마음 싣고
신선처럼 내달은 참꽃 아름 동산
손잡고 꺾어 든 진달래 꽃방망이
파란 입술 마주거울 방긋한 설렘

뒷손 모은 돌담에 함초롬한 볕살
해맑은 소녀의 가냘픈 속삭임에
스치는 시절은 봄눈 속에 저리고
진달래 분홍치마에 뜨거운 노을

부지깽이 끝에 하얀 눈물 날리며
소죽 끓이던 구수한 사랑방 가마
불꽃 흩어진 고즈넉한 옛 마당을
구곡간장 한숨 넘는 진달래 동산

019. 검정 고무신

하얀 고무신만 신겠다고
칭얼대며 가로저었던
아득한 날의 검정 고무신

아이놈 트집에 할아버지 미소는
굽어 타는 연기의 긴 담뱃대로
화롯가만 톡 톡

내려보는 따가운 눈총
못내 지우려
빈 가슴에 끼운 하얀 고무신

검정 고무신 우겨 신고
하얗게 닳도록
들판을 달려 보았어야지

무딘 뒤꿈치로 돌계단을 딛고
다보탑에 기댄 빛바랜 가을에
지붕 위로 까마귀 울어대는데

깨닫지 못한 채 가버린 날들이
시린 손 휘저어
까맣게 타는 하늘

020. 첫정

나는 벌새인가 봐
너를 보면 한없이 가슴이 뛰어

상큼 발랄 고운 새싹 웃음은
풀잎에 맺힌 영롱한 이슬에
알알이 박힌 하늘

사슴도 선녀도 없이 날고픈 날에
성긴 햇살의 풋사과여도
억새 둥지 틀 행복은 연모했는데

굴곡의 파문에 먹구름 고이더니
메아리친 소문이 철렁 내려앉아
벌써 배 떠난 네 심중도 모르고
굽이굽이 낙동강 허전한 원망에
떨구려 견딘 시름이 얼마였던가

돌담을 서성거린 쓰라린 넋은
여태 발그림자 걷지 못하고
아련한 골목에 흔적이나 미울까 봐
숨죽이고 가만히 들추어보니
요란한 빗줄기에 초라히 가린 세월

샘 깊이 품은 벌새 가슴에
첫정은 아직도 목이 마르고
반짝거리던 초록 향기는
쉼 없이 출렁이는 너울이어라

021. 송화강변 미인송(松花江邊 美人松)

송화강 벅찬 물결 우렁찬 달음질
마당마당 도열한 높푸른 깃발은
출정의 땅 울림치는 발해의 함성

평정의 염원 담은 진격의 포효로
광활한 대륙을 포용으로 휘감아
만백성을 보살피는 거룩한 마음

천년을 다잡아 부릅뜬 백산흑수
고이 다져 품은 칼 드높이 들고
뜻 모은 큰 꿈 벌판에 이루리라

북진의 자욱한 힘찬 나팔 소리
불끈 솟아 가득히 밝은 햇살에
초롯초롯 움트는 창창한 기상

말총머리 늠름 미더운 참사랑은
살포시 피운 숨결 구름배 타고
별콩달콩 속삭이는 금빛 강나루

뭉클댄 한 아름 깊이 밴 솔향에
아름다이 발현하는 초록 영웅은
푸른 강물 움켜잡아 말을 달린다

펼치리라 찬란한 민족의 미래
송화강변 가득 훤칠한 미인송
우리의 왕국이 여기에 있었네

022. 고향 풍경

늠름 바위 감돌아 포로록 솟는 샘
어깨동무 도란도란 초련 속삭임에
가재는 힘찬 기지개 돌멩일 어영차
정어린 눈망울 새끼노루 귀를 쫑긋

볏짚단에 떨궈놓은 참새 발자국에
첫서리 하얀 웃음 돌담 위 솔바람
고욤에 잠자리 막내처럼 뱌비대고
다 삭인 홍시는 숨 빨강 풍경소리

뻐근한 황소싸움에 막걸리는 타도
춤추는 고삐에 깊은 시름 훠얼 훨
장독대 정화수에 다소곳이 손잡아
하늘 높이 숭고한 우리 엄마 염원

도토리랑 알밤이 도도록한 마루에
포갠 숯 가슴일랑 원망으로 곧추고
할아버지 회초리가 살아 바른길에
시리도록 푸른 부용자 꽃피는 새월

023. 인연의 굴레

놓아라
놓아버려라
가슴 아픈 인연
밥숟갈 놓듯이

끊어라
끊어버려라
맺지 못할 인연
고무줄 자르듯이

잊어라
잊어버려라
떠나 버린 인연
치매 온 것처럼

아이고
뭐 하려고
그리 애탄 인연
이으려 했던고

그래도
미련 섬으로
굴레 쓴 돛배는
노 저어 앓는다

024. 그 겨울의 달빛

호롱불 끄고 솜이불 당겨 덮던 겨울밤
포르르 문풍지가 속삭거리는 귀띔에
하얀 눈이 쌓여대는 가슴속 다듬질로
환한 띠살문 살며시 찬바람을 에는데

부풀던 눈밭이 허전히 사위어 애틋한 채
문고리를 당기려는 야릇한 찰나에 쏴아
현란히 펼쳐지는 천지창조의 황토 융단

구유도 초가도 담장 너머 천지를 감싸고
눈 가득 가슴 흠뻑 출렁인 미묘한 주황은
회나무 높이 걸터앉아 하늘 껄껄 보름달

천막 아래 몰래 들어간 가설극장 영사기에
한밤 할머니가 곱게 체질한 주톳빛 가루를
사정없이 뿜어 펼치는 찬란한 빛결의 향연

할아버지 기척에 상기된 황홀경을 닮아도
요란한 붉음은 내일 꿈도 똑똑 두드리겠고
알지 못할 훗날 저승에서도 화려할 달 꽃

한겨울을 덮은 황금 달빛을 둘둘 말아다가
너른 마당에 토석담을 넘놀도록 펼쳐두고
내일은 형이랑 커다란 눈사람을 만들어야지
오랜 일기장엔 내내 주황 달빛이 넘실거린다

025. 애수에 갇힌 상념

도화지에 빨간 금붕어 한 마리 그려놓고
눈물을 글썽이는 일곱 살 아이는
까닭 모를 어항 속 참변이 얼마나 야속하였으랴

향 맑은 하얀 꽃에 붕붕 애처로이 누비는 일벌
몹쓸 나무라 동강동강 낫을 들이민 아카시아를
꿀단지에 빠진 도백이 기억을 몰랐으리오
가위바위보로 사랑 다듬어 아련히 펼치던 이파리야

떠나던 기차를 멈춰 청춘을 태워준 칙칙폭폭 유천역
단발머리와 손잡고 뛴 까마득한 날의 낭만 기관사님
그날 한여름 밤의 까만 강물이 하얗게 나풀거릴레라

여름 저무는 사랑마루에 할아버지가 손자를 불러
엄마 갖다 주라는 두 봉지 풍년초의 깊은 무게는
한양 간 지아비에 먹먹 세월 담배 연기 긴 장마야

피는 봄을 만나려 다투어 나오지 않았다면
이리도 오래 버려두고 멀리 가셨을까요
이제는 오히려 날 기다려 오시지 않는 어머니

세월 갉는 낙엽 소리 쓰륵쓰륵 저무는 해거름에
속 모를 내일 속으로 오 수재너 이 노래 부르자
믿는 도낄랑 오로지 믿어야 발등 편히 걸어가지
소귀를 스치는 경에 여물 씹는 눈망울 버거워라

026. 비가 오는데

봄비에
까르르 연두 잎 나폴나폴 짙어가고
간질이는 소식에 내민 손이 젖는다
고향을 돌고 첫사랑을 스친 애수라
한 백날 창문을 두드리면 좋으련만

구슬비는
영롱한 구슬방울 또르륵 굴려 보다
방긋 뽐내고는 얼른 뿌리로 내달고
초자연의 개미는 총총히 집에 들러
흘러 흐른 에너지 굴렁쇠를 돌리네

그런데
어느 날부터 달리 흐느끼는 봄비다
누가 작은 소망에 악플을 달았는지
멍들어 한숨짓고 축 늘어져 떨구니
추슬러도 대책 없이 헛소문만 매워

생기로운 비야
온갖 문을 닫더라도 열어둔 마음에
쏟아지는 빗소리를 새길 줄 알아야
푸른 날의 빗방울 새싹을 피워보지
고운 비가 차마 사탕발림에 울리야

027. 낙엽 지는데

담담한 적막에 툭 떨어지는
성긴 오동잎에 세심 빗소리
그리움은 방울방울 보글거리고
가물가물 여운의 떨궈둔 정이
어깨를 토닥이네

돛배 떠나듯 어둠 가른 잎사귀에
내려앉는 마음 심란키도 한데
머뭇대던 돌담에 건 새끼손가락
어설피 새겨져 몽글거린 결에
너붓너붓 스며드는 쓸쓸한 추상

내일 다시 만날 값이라도
오늘 헤어짐이 애틋한 그예
초혼 산을 내 부딪는 잿빛 기적에
외로워도 설워 말잔 다짐도 잊고
내가 날 울려 낙엽 지는데

호랑이 담배 필 적 갈에 취한 아인
아폴론 신이 되고 싶었다네

지혜도 사랑 앞에 도사리고
자유로운 구속에 젖은 달빛
한 잎 오동에 노 저어 진다

* 자유로운: 나로 말미암은, 나 때문의

028. 유산

계절과 세월이
울퉁불퉁 뒹굴어
뭉게구름 먹구름

할아버지 할머니
아버지와 어머니
가신 그 길

더러 점점이 얼룩은
말 다문 그림에
가을걷이로 흘린 땀

멈추어 돌아보면
아련한 비단길에
아름다운 인연

보이지도 들리지도
알 수도 잡을 수도
바뀌어 없는 그 날

뜰에 선 꼿꼿 난초
영롱한 보랏빛 한 올
비로소 탄성을 자아내고

도저한 기상 환한 얼굴
단사표음 유산에
무뚝뚝하게
머물 듯 가는 햇살

029. 향수

스쳐 지나가지만
마냥 머무르고 싶고
예사로 잊고 살아도
더러 불쑥하는 속내가
쏜살같이 징검다리를 건너던

세 알 산새 둥지 앙증맞아 애련한
할미꽃 꼬부라진 무덤가 동산으로
나물 캐는 소쿠리에 봄 가득 담아
금잔디에 철부지 참따랗게 굴리던

여섯 아름드리 숲속 포구 나무에
굵게도 꼰 새끼줄 긴 그네가
과거로 미래로 바람을 감아 날면
펄럭이는 치맛자락에 아찔하게 웃던

먼 길의 할아버지 기별 기침에
졸던 병아리 쪼르르 마구간 어밀 찾고
후루룩 참새떼가 대추나무를 흔들던

먼 산 보고 절하는 수수께끼의
디딜방아 쿵더쿵 쑥떡에 송기떡
부서지고 덩이지라 디디는 발 맛에
뒤집고 찧는 장단이 척척 맞아가던

감꽃이 필 때부터 별 꿰어 기다린
얼른 따지 않는다며 성난 홍시가
감쪽지를 재촉하여 발그레 담기던

온 동네가 떠들썩한 잔칫날 합환주를
침 묻힌 손가락에 문구멍을 뚫어보고
또래들이랑 신랑각시놀음 소꿉질하던

달도둑 넘나드는 삽짝 안으로
늦저녁 두리상의 구수한 맛이
박산 튀듯 대청마루에 자우룩하던

디딤돌에 가지런히 닳은 고무신에는
하얀 눈꽃이 고향 찾아 젖어 드는데
시집 못 간 이모의 곤지랑 한 자루
아련히 야릇한 구룡족제비가
솜이불에 감기어 밤 두꺼워지던

흥겨운 신명에 어깨춤 으쓱이며
흙먼지 폴폴한 길 앙감질로 내달아
세상 아늑한 엄마 품으로
팔베개에 젖 물고 꿈 들던

아무것도 없어도
온갖 싹이 돋아나는 듯
설날같이 모여들던 그리움이
오붓이 안뜰을 에운 골목으로
흙을 개어 허물어진 담을 쌓고파

*감쪽지: 감을 따려고 노끈을 얽어 만든 기구
*삽짝: 사립문
*박산: 뻥튀기
*곤지랑: 낮은 목소리가 구르듯 소곤거림
*구룡족제비: 여염집 규수를 만나려고 수챗구멍을 드나들던 절간의 중을 빗댄 이야기 속 동물

030. 포석정

남산 솔밭길 푸른 숨소리 등 굽어도
백 년을 열 번 둥둥 혼 깊은 북소리
현란한 햇살로 울울창창 피어오르고
둘러앉은 유상곡수 허허로운 이만치
굽이도는 돌 홈에 유유 품은 포석정

어사주에 부국강병 능히 뜻을 펼치고
성스러운 잔 올려 환읍하고 음복하던
물길 이십이 미터 둥근 복 사적 일호
화랑도 화백회의 통일의 땅 반가운데

근면 자조 협동의 씨를 뿌린 허물에
지기미 카터당한 박통을 애통해하며
신라 역사 지우려다 제 절로 사라진
적개심 가득한 무릴 의연히 품어 온
어제오늘 내일의 북두칠성 하늘이여

포용의 천년이 황포에 부푸는 보름날
잔 위에 시를 띄워 주름 깊은 나그네
천신에 제를 올려 고비를 헤쳐나가니
손잡은 강강수울래 달빛 포갠 포석정
나는 따라 웃는데 시치미를 떼는구려

*유유(幽幽): 깊고 그윽함
*환읍(環揖): 여럿이 빙 둘러서서 읍함
*지기미(知幾微, 知己未): 몹시 못마땅할 때 욕으로 하는 말. 급히 흐려 유추하면 지미가 되고
　　　　　　지김(죽임)의 낌새를 알고 1919 기미 독립운동과 1979 기미 대통령
　　　　　　시해 사건을 앎

031. 다음

처음이 있어서 다음이 있고
  다음의 다음은 아린 끝이라

칼 품은 눈에는
  한 길 속마음도 접시 위의 바다

얽히고설킨 말글이 천지에 쏟아져도
  꼬인 실타래 휘이 던져 풀매

바람에 흔들리거나
  향기에 취하거나
    빛에 홀리지 말고

터득한 날의 바르게 열린 길로
  마련한 다음을 펼쳐야지
    다음이 다음 문을 가두기 전에

다다른 다음 세상
  알 수 없는 다음날은
    무엇이 있어 그다음을 열까

다가온 마침에 까마득한 시작에
  청량한 노을 지그시 스미어
    배꽃을 구르는 먼동의 말똥 미소

032. 옛이응(ㆁ)의 부활

순수한 우리말 다라ㆁ이는 다라잉이 아닌 다라이, 물을 담는 대야
다리미나 다른 사람을 다리잉이아닌 다리ㆁ이로 쓸 수 없어 애타고
ㆁ을 받침으로 쓰면 오대양 육대주로 잘 굴러가는 우리말이 되는데

가디ㆁ마는은 가더니만, 하디ㆁ마는은 하더니만
가래ㆁ이는 가랑이, 알개ㆁ이는 알갱이
가지러ㆁ이는 가지런히, 나라ㆁ이는 나란히
강내ㆁ이는 강냉이 옥수수 맛좋은 하모니카
걸배ㆁ이는 걸뱅이, 거지는 옳게 사는 지혜라
고디ㆁ이는 우렁이 고둥, 꼬재ㆁ이는 꼬챙이
구디ㆁ이는 구덩이, 길게 말하면 구더기
궁디ㆁ이는 궁둥이 방디ㆁ 엉디ㆁ는 엉덩이
깍재ㆁ이는 깍쟁이 약빠르고 인색한 사람, 풍각재ㆁ이는 풍각쟁이
끈티ㆁ이는 끝에, 긍그ㆁ이는 근근히 간신히
노래ㆁ이는 노랑이 수전노
눈티ㆁ이 밤티ㆁ이는 눈 언저리와 알밤, 눈팅이가 밤팅이 되었네
니ㆁ가는 네가, 니ㆁ는은 너는, 니ㆁ빼ㆁ이는 너뿐이
단다ㆁ이는 단단히
대갈빼ㆁ이는 대갈빼기, 대가리는 지혜의 덩어리
돌미ㆁ이 돌삐ㆁ이는 돌멩이
동그라ㆁ이는 둥글게 동글배ㆁ이는 동그라미
두동싸ㆁ이는 두동사니, 윷놀이에서 두 동이 포개어져 가는 말
등시ㆁ이는 등신

마ㅇ이는 망이가 아닌 많이

막디ㅇ이는 막둥이

매리ㅇ이는 매미

멀끄디ㅇ이는 머리끄덩이 머리카락

모리미ㅇ는 모르면서

모티ㅇ는 모퉁이

몸뻬ㅇ이는 몸빼가 아닌 일할 때 입는 고무줄 바지

몽디ㅇ이는 몽둥이

무다ㅇ이는 무단히 아무런 이유 없이

문디ㅇ이 자슥은 이 모자란 녀석, 문디ㅇ이 가시나ㅇ

바ㅇ아는 방에, 바ㅇ아깐은 방앗간

반티ㅇ이는 함지 항아리

배막디ㅇ이는 배막둥이 융통성이 없는 사람

벌개ㅇ이는 벌래

부지깨ㅇ이는 부지깽이

불티ㅇ이는 불똥 불티ㅇ 강산 용암 천지창조

빨개ㅇ이는 빨갱이, 깍재ㅇ이는 약삭빠른 깍쟁이

빼뿌재ㅇ이는 질경이

솔빼ㅇ이는 솔방울

숯껌디ㅇ이는 숯 그을음

씬내ㅇ이는 씬냉이 씀바귀 꼬들빼기

아ㅇ는 그렇구나 긍정의 아ㅇ아

아주무ㅇ이는 아주머니

앉은배ㆁ이는 앉은뱅이, 오금재ㆁ이는 오금쟁이
올채ㆁ이는 올챙이 잔채ㆁ이는 잔챙이
잠티ㆁ이는 잠충이 잠꾸러기
장때ㆁ이는 장땡 가장 좋은 수나 최고
장똘배ㆁ이는 장돌뱅이, 여러 장을 돌며 물건 파는 장수
조디ㆁ이는 주둥이, 조막디ㆁ이는 조막둥이 아주 작은 것
쭉찌ㆁ이는 쭉정이
첩사ㆁ이는 첩사이 첩실, 작은 마누라
칠개ㆁ이는 칡뿌리
코빵배ㆁ이는 코가 막힌 소리를 내는 사람
파래ㆁ이는 파리, 파란
할마ㆁ이는 할머니
호래ㆁ이는 호랑이, 호매ㆁ이는 호미
히ㆁ야는 형아, 긴 세월에 보고 싶은 히ㆁ야

이다지 엄청난 토박이말을 다 못 들출지언정
지금 쓰는 말을 옳게 적지 못하는 안타까움이여
세계로 뻗어가는 길을 넓히는 우리글의 울림소리
옛이응(ㆁ)의 부활로 우리말을 오롯이 살려낼진저

033. 우리의 약진

줄기차게 이어지는 아름다운 금수강산 굳건하여라
고요한 새벽에 우리는 깨어나 넓은 천지를 달리니
찬란한 태양이 어깨 위로 비추어 기쁨이 솟구치네

추워도 아픔을 같이 나누는 따뜻한 마음 지녔으니
봄날은 진달래 가을은 단풍이 철마다 웃음 꽃피고
땀 흘린 푸른 들판에 오곡백과 알차게 여물어가네

반석에 굳센 기둥 하늘이 보살피는 든든한 지붕에
살기 좋은 새마을을 세상에 펼쳐 평화를 이뤄내고
희망의 등불 드높이 들어 모두가 손잡고 나아가자

배우고 익혀 쌓아온 홍익 정신을 만방에 깨우치고
어루만지는 약손으로 슬기롭게 이웃을 지켜나가서
건강한 참 빛으로 온 누리를 풍요롭게 만들어가자

034. 수수께끼 세상

물 없는 물레방아는?
돌지 않는 네 방아요
레알?

지구는 무엇으로 돌아갈까요?
돈이요
딩 돈 댕!

마음은 어떻게 생겼을까요?
간사의 다이아몬드요
모난 아픔도 둥글면 나을 텐데

아주머니 주머니에 담긴 것은?
아, 염낭엔 나요
난 욕심과 질투의 쩐 서린 비수라오

아저씨는 무엇을 믿을까요?
빽이요
돈줄 놓칠세라 눈두덩이 불룩하구려

열심히 일하면 따라오는 돈이라는데
배움 방송 여론 의원 벼슬 원수 독립
하나같이 매달려 삐딱한 뜀박질이다

길 아닌 길을 멈출 만도 하련만
세상 참 잘 돌아간다?

멎은 물방앗간에 손자는 재롱인데
쭈글 손이 아려오는 남루한 금낭으로
몰려오는 먹구름이 노아의 비를 뿌릴레라
곧 녹아내릴 아이스께끼!

035. 선택사항

화려한 휴식을 찾아 나는 붕어하겠소
승하나 선화가 꽃밭을 지나왔을까마는
돌아가시고 서거에 영면에 소천하시고
하늘나라로 떠나시고 선종에 잠드시고
순직 자결 별세 작고 타계 임종 하직
불귀객 꼬꾸라지고 입적 열반에 들어
숨지고 뒈지고 죽는 생이 한스러운데

백지 모퉁이에 사망이라 빈칸을 메워
호피도 아닌 흔적이라고 남겨두고
흩어지는 진혼곡

모두가 다르게 태어나듯
가는 길이 서로 달라
명경대에 서기까진 모르는 곳을

우러러보아 천당에 말 많아 지옥으로
부끄러운 죽음이 아니기를
살아생전에 고를 수 있도록
임은 어떤 삶을 마감하고플까요

하기야 잘 고른다 해도
둘러선 마음들이 돌아앉으면
맴돈 허공에 산을 넘는 유에프오려니

가서도 숨 쉴 걱정일랑 붙들어 매고
마른 잎의 영롱한 이슬처럼
거짓 없이 살았노라 푸른 하늘에
한 천년쯤 가끔은 정이 새롭도록
마치는 선택사항은 여태 기다린다오

036. 말맛

안녕이라는 인사는 급히 엿보는 듯하여
밥 먹었나 보다 메마른 정에 떨떠름하고
방가보다도 감칠맛이 덜한 터에

코스타리카의 푸라 비다는
잘될 것 같은 인생의 풍요로운 희망에
행복의 푸른 비를 내리듯 여유로운데

스페인의 아디오스는
무심히 스치는 작별마저 허무한 귓전에
쓰리고 아린 이별 맛이 뚝 뚝 떨어지네

이스터섬의 석상 모아이는
지아비를 기리는 수릿재의 망부석이 통곡하듯
어머니를 기리는 애절한 몸부림의 망모석이라

이제 가면 언제 오나 애호 애호 애호남차 애호
혼을 달래는 슬픔이 상여를 부여잡는 산기슭에는
쏟아지는 함박눈에 홍매의 붉은 숨결 잔혹하여라

말 없는 말 따스한 정이 언 마음을 녹이고
참맛은 처음처럼 오롯이 담겨 변치 않는데
숱한 낱말을 덧없이 지저귀는 앵무새 무새

애처로운 우리의 속 깊이 영근 사랑이여
입 밖의 말맛은 순간에 흩어져 허황하니
떠나기까지는 변치 말고 꼬옥 품어둠세

037. 마지막

내일 우리 다시 만날지라도
오늘 헤어지기가 못내 섭섭하기는
가냘픈 구름이 달빛을 옮긴 까닭이요
남은 술을 빈 잔에 못 따른 까닭이요
여린 마음이 보슬비에 젖는 까닭이요
차마 당신을 잊지 못하기 때문이지요
어쩜 이 순간 마지막일지도 모르고요

사물이나 사람이나 그 어떤 마지막도
아직이야 가끔은 못 잊어 그립겠지만
가물가물 바람도 없이 까아만 날이면
못 잊어 못 잊은 가슴에 하늘도 메고

영화의 마지막이 그리 허무한 것은
제 갈 길로 떠나버린 주인공이나
하얀 갈매기에 텅 빈 여운뿐이리오

비슬산에 올라 낙동강을 바라보니
산을 감돈 강은 끝내 끝을 흐리어
보일 듯 보지 말라며 가리는 연무

주렁주렁 대추가 붉게 여물어
맑은 기운의 탄생을 속삭여도
이제 세상을 놔주련다는 손에
작별의 인사가 얼마나 힘든지
마지막이라는 말은 참 슬퍼요

마지막
그 순간만은 오지 않기를
가만히 눈감아보는 비원이라오

038. 베짱이

실톱으로 야금야금 별 다듬는 꽃밭
베틀 장단 지그시 거문고를 뜯어
살근살근 명주 짜는 흥겨운 가락

브읍 브읍 법 없는 법에
넉넉한 한 가닥 어둠을 두들기니
하얀 꽃잎 수줍어 가린 면사포
쿵더쿵 덩더꿍 마음을 찧네

풀벌레 울음이 쓰리지 않았다면
여윈 달은 어찌 다시 피어나
한 많은 고개를 넘었으리오

세상은 염원의 끝에 달려있었네
굽히지 아니하고 버티는 성품에
부지런히 갈고닦아 바르게 펴고

젊어 산 고생 끝에 늙어 꽃피우며
번성하는 가문에 베풀고 여유롭게
두둑한 배짱의 베짱이로 살아야지

훨훨 꿈 펴는 오늘 밤에는
별빛 소곤거리는 꽃밭에서
남몰래 오롯이 이루어놓은
자신만만한 뒷짐 지고
하늘을 튕기는 베짱이 배짱

039. 수를 찾아서

처음엔 누런 봉투가 얇아도 좋아라
한 달에 한 번씩 수고했다고 받았는데
어느 날부터 돈은 냄새만 풍기고
예금통장에 숫자로 그려졌었지

두 다리가 잘나가던 시절에는
이곳저곳에 어설피 그 수를 나누었는데
후다닥 동강 난 몫에는 알다시피
동그라미가 자꾸만 여위어 가네

과부 사정 과부가 모른달 수야
나눌 곳을 보아 더 많이 모아야 하는데
외로워지는 영의 짙어지는 한숨에
어쩌나 갈 길 먼데 날은 저물고

수가 아니라지만 영은 동글어서
무너진 하늘에도 솟을 구멍이 있다기에
노다지 굴을 찾아 산길로 접어드니
무리수를 둔다 하네 속도 모리미

* 모리미: 모르면서의 천 년 전 표준말

040. 물수제비뜨기

잔잔한 냇가에 책가방을 내려놓고
납작한 돌멩이를 슬기롭게 던지면
사뿐사뿐 물을 걷는 어여쁜 나비
너는 다섯 번 나는 그만 풍덩
물수제비뜨는 내기에 빠진 즐거움

모서리를 잡은 검지에 힘주어
옆으로 몸을 굽혀 팔매질하면
도깨비 뛰듯 팔딱이는 곡예에
생각도 하늘도 무아경에 들고
물방울은 하얀 손뼉 반짝반짝

물수제비 날렵하게 흩날린 날이
낯설게 흐르는 물을 박차고
나 여기 있다며
말간 얼굴 내미는 어디쯤에서

쪼끄만 돌멩이 하나 꼭 쥐고
튀어 오르는 물수제비가
더없이 맛난 오늘

함박눈도 머춤하는 가지 사이로
송이송이 눈수제비
초록 꿈을 뜬다

041. 변화의 정신문명

사랑의 온기가 꽉 차는 자그만 집에
수수한 옷차림 빈약한 밥상을 즐기고
버스 지하철 왕성한 걸음에 건강하게

『실수해도 손가락질 대신 격려하고
조금 알더라도 공부하고 노력하며
자기는 낮추고 상대방을 존중하며
예의로 깍듯이 귀천 없이 대하고

탈세하지 않고 정직하게 근검절약하고
대안으로 비판하되 진정한 애국자 되고
조언을 경청하고 협심해서 일 처리하며
잘못은 서로 책임지고 나라를 자랑하며
여럿이 하는 일에는 뭉치고 단결하여』
세상에 가장 아름다운 민족이 되도록

목숨 바쳐 백성 구할 위인은 잠겨도
이렇게 되는 나라로 품어본 희망이요

변화를 외쳐대는 시대에 진정한 것은
남 먼저 내가 이렇게 사는 것일진대
국민을 편안케 하려는 마음가짐을
사회적 통념의 가치로 지켜가야지요

74

042. 고독한 바람

밥을 먹다가
혹여 창조자 지팡이 짚고 서 계실까
바라본 하늘

기러기 떠나 메마른 노을
양떼구름 쉬는 틈 사이로
한두 번 보일만도 하련만
하느님 참 게으른가 보다
품어 지난 두 천년에 하얀 섶이라도

피조물이 더러워지면 곧 씻을만한데
아직 쉴만하고 때가 덜 탄 세상일세
정화의 빗자루로 말끔하게 걷어내고
세게 쳐야지 팽팽 바르게 도는 우주

관악산 위로 풍덩 백상아리 한 마리
실동태에 그 뼈 달고 신나 달렸는데
깜빡할 새 로켓으로 임 마중 가는군

어디에 숨었나 푸르른 꿈의 까꿍 별
천리안도 심봉사에 외로운 숨바꼭질
사색으로 지새우다 한 획을 치는 빛

고운 고난 아프게 견딘 독립불구에
누구 있나 어디 같이 밥 먹을 사람
백지장 들고
갈망 문풍지

043. 행복을 펼치는 수업

행복하게 살기를 원해도 행복한 삶이 무엇에 달렸는지는 모르지
소중한 하나가 나날을 아프지 않게 사는 것인데
먼 훗날 낯도 선 병원에 아픈 몸을 맡길 생각뿐
누구도 어린 시절 꿈싹을 길러주려 하지 않았네

의사 가운에 청진기를 들고 구급용 가방을 여는 병원놀이 아이들
내 손은 약손 네 배는 똥배라 쓰다듬는 할머니
무속에도 난치병을 고치는 치병 능력을 갖는데
자신의 몸을 자기만큼 잘 아는 의사가 없을 터

초등시절부터 한두 가지 이상의 의술을 습득하도록 초석을 놓아
누구나 밥 먹듯 병을 돌보는 의사가 될 수 있도록
소꿉놀이 치료 재능을 꾸준히 키워주면 될 터인데

모든 이가 필수과목으로 이수케 하여 만백성이 의사 되는 그날에
'호' 해주는 딸의 온기에 마음의 통증도 사라지고
창궐하는 병마는 얼씬 못 하게 스스로 구원하도록
인류여, 소싯적부터 전 국민의료교육을 시행함이 마땅치 않겠소?

오진 횡포 집단이기 의료비 누수 막고
올바로 된 성 지식을 함양토록 알리며
의사란 기본 직업에 다른 일자리 얹어
아무도 안 아프고 모두 부유해지도록!

044. 음모에 둘린 궤

낮말을 주워들은 멧비둘기는
세월 속 칠 각의 당나귀 임금 귀라
절레절레 아홉 번을 울어 젖히고

밤말을 훔쳐 들은 까만 쥐새끼
도둑고양이 앞에서 털어놓을까
공주의 휘둘린 참 궤 얘기를

적폐로 조작한 증삼살인에
침소봉대로 억울을 덧씌워
바른길에는 인적도 드문데

중상모략이 흔드는 도깨비불에
이리로 우르르 저리로 좌르르
고픈 잉어 떼 빈손 따라 허둥지껄

어둠의 갈퀴에 갇힌 솔깃 귀
쪼개진 눈길과 가슴 사이로
스멀스멀 안개 치는 악마의 덫니

뚜벅이 황소가 긴 꼬리 휘둘러도
음결로 뜨는 모기를 척결치 못해
뭉쳐야 산다는 참뜻을 안다면
깨어있는 머리는 모두 맞대고

음모에 둘린 궤 올바로 열어
공주는 금반지 하나
음모는 은팔찌 둘

045. 뻐꾸새

뱁새 둥지에 잽싸게 알 밀어 넣고 뻐꾹
딱새 둥지에 떡하니 알 쑤셔 넣고 뻐꾹
나 너 몰라 돌아앉아 시치미 떼는 뻐꾹
숨 막히고 속 타는 봄날의 뻐꾸새 뻐꾹

고로쇠 빨아 먹는 고무관을 빼버린다고
하이에나가 나랏돈을 제자리로 옮길까
뼈아픈 희생자의 위로금 위에 걸터앉아
정의로운 듯 무게 잡고 개빈다리 뻐꾹

삐딱한 세상은 속이며 살아야 한다던가
덕지덕지 가리고 파묻고 덧씌운 진실에
잘 키워줘 고맙긴커녕 약 오르지 뻐꾹
방귀 뀐 놈이 성내는 우중충한 뻐꾹

군림을 품고 겉 봉사하는 얼빠진 도둑에
그 아비에 그 자식이라 썩어간 적반하장
희한하게 맞장구쳐대는 끔뻑끔뻑 뻐꾹
유전자 검사 안 해도 뻔한 금붕어 뻐꾹

십자가는 뻐끔하며 붉은 피를 토하고
황포돛배 공양미에 검게도 찢어지네
쑥쑥국 쑥국 참꽃은 언제나 피어나고
만들지 않으면 된 날이 오긴 하려나
보리밭에 처연한 뻐꾸기 뻑뻐꾹 뻐꾹

046. 스테인리스스틸

슬지 않는다는 스테인리스강에 녹이 슬고
순도가 포나인인 금덩일 순금이라 한다네
영구적이란 것들이 반영구도 아닐뿐더러
고장 나면 고치지도 못하는 고물이 되고
백 프로 참 재료의 비율은 오리무중이요
하나의 평생도 겨우 백수에 머무는데
그마저 아흔아홉이라며 한 살을 깎네

대통합을 웨던 통령이 분열의 이정표니
철석같이 다진 말은 담 넘은 구렁이요
태평성대 뒷감당에 백성이나 성가시고
뽑아준 마음을 우습게 여기는 꼬라지라
백로는 감춰둔 복장으로 어지럽혀 돌고
겉 희고 속 검어 잿빛 되는 방방곡곡에
사랑을 울리고 배반으로 삼켜 팽개치네

나이깨나 먹은 세상이 나잇값을 하려도
욕심으로 물든 파도는 너울로 덮쳐오고
배려는 길 건너 붉은 신호등에 묶여있어
하나로 묶을까 셋으로 쪼갤까 갈라진 혀

저엇대 하나로 녹 없는 놋쇠를 두들기니
가버린 모두는 하염없이 애달픈 진실에
토 안 단 세월 부지런히 달궈 넘기라네

자유의 만끽엔 책임과 제약이 배꼽이요
꼭 잠근 수도꼭지에 또옥 똑 물방울은
삶을 낭비한 여백의 애끓는 덤이로구려

047. 전봇대

먼 산 보고파 높이선 동구 전봇대에
졸랑졸랑 검둥이는 뒷다리를 치켜들어 씩 웃고
비틀비틀 다가온 아이 부르르 반가운 듯 안더니
바지를 추스르고는 잘 자라라는 인사도 없네

차를 몰고 온 아낙이 선사하는 큰 짐보따리에
대머리 신사는 낡은 봉지 하나를 툭 던져두고
빈손을 털고는 하늘 한 번 쳐다보는데
비는 오려나 우레가 치려나

멋진 장갑 검은 마스크의 긴 머리 여인
네모난 종이 척 붙이고는 종종걸음이고
어디서 씩씩거리며 다가온 젊은 녀석의
느닷없는 발길질이 고수는 아닌가 보다

장마 구름을 이고 축 처진 날에
전봇대는 윙윙 한숨으로 여위어 가고
갈 길 없는 낙엽마저 위로의 꿈을 보태네

어깨띠의 한 무리가 긁어 뗀 누더기가
하얀 가루 나비가 되어 떠나가는 길에
잘난 모습 붙였던 의원은 축가를 불렀을지
바람은 또 재개발 삽을 뜨는 헌 신도시로
죄없이 긴 전봇대를 휘감아 돌아
칼날 같은 바람에 묻히는 계절에
산은 키 작은 전봇대를 나무라고 있네

048. 아파트

아파트가 아파 터진다고 꿈틀대니
머리가 지끈하고 가슴도 답답구려

사라진 성냥갑 여기 다 쌓이는 듯
자꾸 높이 올라가는 고소공포증에
가치도 월급도 훌쩍한 억 투기에
일조권 조망권 갈취세에 투덜투덜
곰팡이에 줄줄 새고 시끌벅적한데
기우뚱 우당탕 남이 지은 집이라

코린트에 르네상스식은 아니더라도
집은 편안하게 사는 맛이 있어야지
저 아픈 아파트에 누가 기거하는지
상식도 질서의 문도 위기에 걸렸고
그 흔한 강남아파트도 사주지 못해
아이놈 원망 소리 사무치게 찌르네

땅을 울리는 재개발 어느 방향인지
내용 연수 들먹이며 수명을 줄이고
발 빠른 정보 장사 천금의 곰 발에
속상한 개는 지붕도 못 쳐다보는데
일회용 같은 아파트에 녹슨 발걸음
뼈아픈 가치관에 아픈 미련만 가득

정든 초가삼간 감자 굽는 굴뚝은
초라한 꿈이 너무 많이 타버려서
오래도록 잠도 오지 않는가 보오

049. 격차

백지 한 장 집어 들고 갑부가 내민 억
백금으로 만든 거예요
멋있게 청혼문을 쓸 거예요
망치면 그냥 버려야죠
주려면 안 가져가지만 내놓으면 금방 없어져요

안목에 그만한 가치를 인정하니까 샀다고
명품손수건 한 장에 천만 원이라나
이별이 비싸서 좋을까만
눈물을 닦고 버릴 거예요
아픈 나라로 가겠죠

유기농 사과는 한 개에 삼천만 원이요
임을 위해서라면 이 정도는 아무것도 아니에요
농사지은 사람도 대우를 받아야죠
속이 썩은 줄도 모르고 말거나
잘 보면 알 터인데도 아는 사람이

이 집은 몇조밖에 안 해요
비가 새면 밀어버리고 다시 지어야죠
우리 식구가 살 집인데 잘 지어 오래 살아야죠
무너진 기둥에 풍비박산 난 펀드꾼의
식모와 경비원은 어디로 안타까운데

격이 다른 꿈이라서 다행이다 참
천 원으로 물과 라면을 아직은 살 수 있고
백 원에 다섯 장을 샀으니 엄청 부자지요

050. 용꿈의 함정

용꿈을 꾸지 마라
용이 있었다손 치더라도 사라진 동물에
용은 간신배들의 노리개였어
용용 죽겠지, 제아무리 용해도
용은 그럴듯하게 상상이 빚은 것으로
육룡이 나르샤 여의주나 희롱했겠거니
백성의 마음을 빼앗으려 가공하였나니
꿈 시절에는 누구나 용이 되려 했지만

봉황 꿈도 꾸지 마라
봉이 있었다손 하더라도 더는 못 볼 터
봉은 여인네를 현혹하려 만들었다네
봉이 되지 말거니와 봉을 잡지도 말게
좋을 듯한 귀한 일이 정말 좋을까다
봉창 두드리는 소릴랑 자다가도 접게
치맛자락에 병아리 냄새가 나약하니
물 찬 제비가 봉황보다 어여쁜 날일세

지렁이를 용이라 닭 꿈을 봉황이라 하면
하는 거야 못 말리는 오래된 궁전에서
후덥지근한 날 용봉탕이나 한 그릇 하세

용꿈으로 로또 한 장을 사고 싶은 밤이나
꿈을 움직일 수 있다면 정신이 맑다 하니
등용문의 힘든 야망일랑 책상에 펼쳐두고
겁 없이 배회하다 수풀 밑에 머문 꿈으로
시원한 몸부림 둥실둥실 용틀임의 두둥실

051. TV를 켜면

TV를 켜면
내일 다시 만나자며 한참 손을 젓거나
돼지 멱 따는 감탄사만 요란 벅적지근한데
아프면 병원에 가라는 하얀 옷이 허접하고
요란한 광고에 채널을 돌리는 헛수고까지

하늘에 없는 비를 뿌리는 예보는 나라를 닮았고
떡 먹는 뭉게구름 꼬리를 잡아 내일을 흔드는데
사람 소리 노랫소리가 숨죽인 입술에 요상터니
삐뚠 악기 거친 소리가 목소릴 삼켜 귀가 타네
미술에도 명상에도 고된 음악이 울고 앉았으리

초를 칠한 사실에 비틀어 끄는 아나운서에
양분된 패널은 귀신 씻나락 까먹는 궤변에
저쪽 끝에 앉아 갈 데까지 가자는 연극에
악다구니 말싸움에는 잡초마저 시무룩해져

군더더기 없이 정화된 아름다운 목소리에
판단력을 턴 사실의 참 전달이 언제리오

돈만 보고 악만 질러대는 네모상자에는
걸 따라 개 짖는 소리만 왁자지껄하니
허튼 전기요금이나 아껴야지

아파하다 보니 화면이 쪼개져 버렸네
이를 어쩌나 반창고로 붙일 수도 없고
며칠 새 백만 원이 폐기물 되는 아쉬움에
TV를 끈다

052. 여소치(仔笑齒)

웃는 치아가 참하게 보인다면
세상을 한참 덜 살았노라고
하얀 어둠이 까맣게 웃겠네

경멸과 저주를 깊이 품은 조소에
속 달리 눈치 보는 여소치의 함정
웃는 여자가 다 예쁘다고 생각지 마라
웃는 남자가 다 친절하다 여기지 마라

낯선 길손에게 다른 길을 알려주어
지나온 길이 공허한데
아름답게 웃는 치아를 정말 모를레라
비뚤어진 천사가 저럴레라

간첩 신고는 흔적도 없고
유발한 실수는 번개처럼 꼬집는데
봄비에 젖는 묘한 미소에
일그러진 하늘을 조롱하는 여소치

웃는 모습에 그만 침을 꿀꺽하고
소리장도 알 수 없는 가면 너머로
모름을 모르는 이 그 얼마리요

053. 동물원의 구성요소

도리 없는 망치를 들고 앉아
현장을 조사도 없이 아는 듯한 심판이
어긋난 잣대를 허투루 들이대고
도깨비방망이를 덩더쿵 쿵더쿵

돌린 고개로 눈 감고 두드리는
상식도 팽개치고 덕도 없이 희한한 권력
무리의 내 편만 내 동물이라
군지렁 시부렁 도깨비방망이

편리한 내 입맛에 조령모개로
내일 또 우리 맘대로 뜯어고치면 된다네
동물들이 뽑은 선량인데 누가 알랴
맞장구에 방망이 얼씨구나 좋다

오만한 동물원도 손안의 명경인데
정신없이 따르는 무리의 도깨비방망이
세 개의 방망이가 설치고 있다
똥 나와라 뚝딱 나 몰라라 뚝딱

정갈한 마음에 깨끗깨끗 손 팔 들고
손바닥에 얹힌 동물원의 구성요소
도깨비야 물러가고 금 나와라 뚝딱
우리 우리에는 천도복숭아가 열리리라

054. 골동품

케케묵은 세상 사람이라고?
웃기지 마라
이미 알아차린 미소니라

배타적인 개인영웅주의에 빠진 권력으로
늙은이에게 물어보지도 않고
함부로 불합리한 노인 권익 다투지 마라
먼 듯한 깨칠 날이 돌차간이네

가마때기라서 가만히 있는 것이 아닐세
가짠키는 할지언정 일말의 기대감이지

오래되고 희귀한 세간품 하나를
시대 감각 잃은 무딘 물건 취급 안 하고
부모보다 잘 모시는 집도 더러 있더라만

반듯한 가문의 온고지신 번영에
청출어람 청어람을 누가 바라지 않으랴
골동품은 어지러운 가치에 견딜 뿐이지
죽두목설이 어디 하찮기만 하겠는가?

*가짠타: 어이없는 모양과 행동을 볼 때 하는 말

055. 신념의 공간

빛과 바람과 소리는
무게도 없는데 마음을 누르고
유령의 얼굴로 간담이 서늘해

팔꿈치를 굽힐 만한 머리맡에
여유로운 신념의 공간을 두고
혹시 휘둘릴지도 모를
가치 없는 무게와
진실 가린 얼굴에
가차 없는 잣대를 들어야지

억수 같은 장마에
사라호 태풍은 부숴대고
새벽 전화 소리가
애잔한 상여의 초혼인데

토란잎에 물방울이 똘방똘방하듯
팔베개에 대가리를 뒤척거려보는
오래된 잣대의 굽은 신념 공간에
좨드는 시간 속 움츠린 옴나위로
지푸라기만큼의 자유를 뻗어보네

*대가리(大伽利): 지혜 덩어리, 두부 전체

056. 일관성

포은의 돌다리는 아직 붉은데
훈민정음에 파묻힌 위화도회군
허망한 국치에 분단을 낳고만
원죄를 모르쇠로 어물쩍댈쏜가

어설픈 천년이 더 지나기 전에
요동 정벌에 대마도를 되찾아
정죄로 바로 세워 가야 할진저

배반의 동족상잔에 인색한 포용
사색당파 민욕 빨갱이에 휘둘려
편협과 배타의 싹만 키우다가
찢어지고 잃었던 어지러운 땅

역성혁명 동학혁명 오일육혁명을
혓바닥의 이율배반 삐뚠 잣대로
지우개에 시달린 민족은 아픈데

남들은 아름다운 고려라 하건만
통일도 저 멀리 오만 년 역사를
오천 년 세월이라 자랑하고플까

살아남은 모두 같이 당한 친일에
이불속의 독립 만세 독립군 되어
침략자엔 한주먹 응징도 못 하고
애먼 겨레 몰아서 독풀이 해대면
패배의 민심만 눈 흘기는 한강아

뜻 모아 건너야 할 숱한 갈래에
야릇하게 편 가르는 검은 앨리스
차려야 할 일관성 불타는 선죽교

057. 총알을 막는 법

판결에 수 세월 판단도 아리송해
상식을 뒤집는 선고에 불끈 주먹
법이 어려워 재판이 해석한 오류
들어도 보지 않고 글자에 망치만

사법이 쩔쩔매는 난해한 법조문
내 병 고치는 의사 하나 없듯이
법 모르는 법조인이 수도 없는데

너 나 쉬이 알게 바르게 펼치어
올바른 잣대가 아름다운 나라에
법망을 빠져나가는 법이 없도록

북에서는 남으로 큰 총을 겨누고
남에는 서로가 말 총을 쏴대는데
외침이 빗발치는 날이 오기 전에
총알 막는 법이라도 굳게 에워야
지 다 죽고 나면 뉘 법정에 서랴

감추려 통계의 함정도 파지 말고
분명한 심증이면 물증 탓을 마라
레닌 쓰레기 쿵쿵대는 개도 없게
상식을 넘보지 않는 법을 지키자

058. 계단

알밴 다리 끌고 오르는 돌계단에는
참 많은 바람이 고개를 숙이고 있어
병자의 치유 연인의 사랑 취업 합격

두 계단을 올라가 소원을 이룬다면
밟아온 계단에 원망이야 남을쏜가
할머니는 무슨 죄로 돌을 쓰다듬네

계단에 떠오르는 다단계의 먹구름이
거치는 단계마다 돈 거머리 사기로
무너지는 현장에는 자욱한 아우성만

단계의 꼭대기는 낄낄대는 비굴함
지나는 단계에는 뼈를 깎는 비린내
피 부르는 아픔만 다단계로 쌓이네

돌계단에 다단계가 괴롭히는 것은
행복을 위해 힘들게 오르는 땀에
갓바위의 영험하단 약 때문이라오

꼬드기는 단계가 자꾸 속일지라도
굳건한 돌계단 아름답게 디뎌 올라
못 이룬 금의환향 꼭 성취하옵소서

059. 개새끼(皆子息)

사람의 새끼가 되고 나서부터
다 같은 자식의 개자식이라도
부르기가 어설픈 이름 개새끼

변하다 보니 개인지 사람인지
같은 철부지로 침침한 회삭에
부모는 개처럼 개는 자식같이
계면 활성제도 지친 경계에서

선동질 해코지에 미움이 쌓이고
밥 주는 양친 손을 물기도 하여
무작한 개차반이란 비난을 사서
쓰라린 냉가슴이 나무란 개새끼

돼지 새끼 애저는 잘도 먹건만
곁 눈치 힘겨운 전통의 개장국
설치는 팬데믹 안개 속 치료에
몹쓸 죄 집단이기 짓는 개느님

목줄 풀린 개새끼 천방지축으로
인간이 어버이라고 설쳐 덤비니
개사람의 이빨은 누가 감당할꼬
달을 짖는 개 슬 꼬랑질 감추네

자 그만 사람 벗어 개자리 찾고
개새끼가 없는 땅 지상낙원으로
배려의 쉼터 코리아를 만들고저

060. 붕어가 상어를 이기려면

붕어가 상어를 이기려면
민물로 끌어들인다
많이 모여 같이 덤빈다
번개처럼 급소를 찌른다
다른 상어에게 돈을 준다

여의치 않아
신의 도움을 청한다
북의 핵폭탄을 상어 목에 단다

지느러미가 보약이라 퍼뜨린다
그래 그거야 어시
천적이 그 흔한 인간인 걸
왜 진작 알았어야지

허
야기요단이로세
강태공도 아닌 저 사람
샥스핀은 제쳐두고
붕어를 찝쩍이네

*어시: 물고기 지느러미

061. 맷돌과 까마귀

높아 못 따먹고 남 주기 아깝고
찔러본 심술이 남긴 까치밥인데
까치도 먹다 둔 맛 처진 홍시를
알뜰히도 나누어 먹는 까마귀는
물병에 돌을 채우는 영특함으로
초상난 집을 귀신같이 알려주니
얼마나 지혜로운 까망 마귀일까

욕심이 빠뜨린 바다의 소금 맷돌
오늘도 짠 땀을 흘리며 돌아가리
숱한 탐욕에 퇴색하는 물과 소금

사랑할 감 좋은 감나무의 까마귀
바닷속 맷돌을 얼른 물고 나오면
고혈압 염려 놓는 깨끗한 소금에
먹을 물 걱정 없는 세상 될 텐데

갈 곳 없이 덥고 짜증이 날 때는
젖꼭지에 침을 발라 부채 부치던
지혜의 언행을 온 세상에 나누며
매에 반짝거리는 깜장 날개 위로
까악 까악 슬기의 장을 펼쳐보리

062. 법인

인격체를 부여한 법인의 구성원
그들의 생명을 제한해야 할까요

다툰 경쟁에서 가족이 되었는데
주인처럼 일하는 청춘의 직장에
잘못이 없으면 평생을 일궈야지

명퇴에 정년에 구조조정이라면서
긴 삶을 싹둑 잘라 내동댕이치면
가정도 법인도 사회도 정상일까?

한 사람의 인재를 골라 뽑았으면
사후는 몰라도 힘든 노후 병까지
앗아간 선택시간 보장해주어야지
굳이 떠나겠다면야 할 수 없지만

얄팍한 술수 경쟁의 틀을 벗어나
사람이 살도록 법인 법을 바꿔야
고요한 아침을 만들 수 있잖겠소

다 받아들이는 바다 같은 포용에
굳건한 신뢰의 흔들림 없는 사회
내일 세상 바른 나라를 만들려면
올바른 제도라야만 하지 않겠소?

명동을 오가는 수많은 사람 중에
얼마나 애탄 유령이 섞여 우는지
코스모스백화점 무법 블랙홀에는
손을 뻗은 별들이 빨려들고 있소

063. 예의 바른 나라라

내 하나 물어볼게
니는 예의가 바르다고 생각하나?
그러면 다른 사람은 예의가 바르나
그런데 무슨 촛대뼈나 까겠노
예의도 없는 착각에 빠져 있제

정계나 클럽이나 구석에서 삐딱하고
용서해주고 보니 또한 배신스럽지
그런데 무슨 예의를 바라겠노
그 아비에 오염된 그 자식이지

보이는 곳에서는 잘난 척하더니만
으슥한 데서는 시커먼 짓 다 하고
돈과 권력 탐할 때는 머릴 조아려도
꾼 돈 떼어먹는 뻔뻔한 다반사에
어수룩한 등골을 빼먹는 풍토여

젊은이는 고기를 늙은이는 뼈를 뜯는
끝내는 칠십 고려장의 공자님이
예의 있는 나라로 이끌려 한 말씀을
아전인수 자가당착에 견강부회하여
얼렁뚱땅 넘어가는 예의 없는 나라

알면서 그러면 더 삐뚤겠지만
몰랐다면 지금이라도 고쳐먹고
외지인이 속내를 알면 창피도 하여
예의가 뭔지 물어보면 기가 막히네
화끈대며 가르쳐도 알아는 차려야지

동방의 등불 기울어 희미한데
예의지국 만들기가 그리 쉽겠나!

064. 사랑의 승화 호흡 – 설원 선생님 隨息觀을 새겨

헛된 고백성사 무량으로 한들
생각만으로 짓는 죄에 묻히니
꿈틀대는 욕망 얄궂은 속내가
진흙을 헤어나 연꽃으로 피듯

충동이 화산처럼 치밀어올 때
성욕을 제어하는 수식관 호흡
숨이 드나드는 코끝을 응시해
고요히 열까지만 숨 세어보렴

범코도 싫고 안 된다는 생각에
숨 쉴 자세로의 바뀜이 힘들지
쥐도 새도 모르게 사르르 풀린
환희를 맛본다네 셋도 안 되어

가다듬고 들숨 날숨 숨을 느껴
긍정도 부정도 하지 말고 보면
깨달음도 코앞의 여반장이라네

숨으로 이기면 살아나는 내 몸
성으로부터의 벗음이 해탈이라
스님도 신부도 다다를 줄 모른
초월의 경지가 바로 여기 있지

어설픈 성교육 앓는 죄책감에
너나없이 척하며 내빼지 말고
사랑을 순수로 승화하는 호흡
숨을 보며 고통을 떨쳐버리세

결가부좌로 미간에 달이 뜨면
맑은 마음속에는 해가 환하네

065. 매미

굼벙굼벙 뒹굴어 칠 년을 견디다
맹~
첫아들 세상 깨듯
타잔이 밀림을 가르듯
티 없는 마음을 말갛게 울린다

환골탈태에 하얀 선퇴 벗어두고
푸른 수훈 야금야금 이레를 펼치어
더위를 사르고 간 배려의 공간에는
오덕의 익선관이 선명하여라

하늘을 오를 듯 매미 허물에는
아토피 백내장 중이염을 다스린
굼벵이의 덕이 서려 있음을

똑 떨어지는 청량한 한 줄기
매미나 꽃이나 이슬방울같이
짧은 흔적을 거두어갈지언정

맴 맴 맴 맴 맹~
사라져가는 내 탓의 영웅은
한참이나 마음을 토닥인다오

066. 운명의 존재

한 올의 털이 몸통을 흔드는
운명을 노력도 어쩔 수 없지
닥치는 괴롬은 운명의 존재여도
눈썹 위에 수수방관 후 후 팔짱

목숨을 던질 만큼 베푼다면
운명을 바꿀 수도 있다지만
시절의 흐름에 맞추어 따르라고
뜻은 일찌감치 정해져 있었다네

약이 병을 못 고치거니와
병이 사람을 못 잡아가니
음양관계 조절로 양기를 기르고
때로 굶어보면 살길도 있으련만
고파 죽느니 먹어 고치겠다 하니

풍수 철학 신봉에 천묘의 발복에
섬긴 신을 찾아 위안을 받는대도
안타까이 아리는 운명의 꼭두각시
지은 대로 가는 걸 알쯤엔 늦다네

067. 티 없는 배려심

에어컨을 켜면 시원보다 먼저
묻은 먼지가 유령의 춤사위고
쏙 뽑은 티슈 나부끼는 티끌이
지구를 뒤덮어대는 화산재인데
아는지도 모른 척 입을 훔치네

사원 식당에서 먼저 먹은 상사가
벗어놓은 옷을 툴툴 털어 입고서
한참 둘둘 뗀 두루마리 화장지에
괜한 물기를 닦고는 휙 아까운데
내 것 아닌 이전에 속 타는 먼지

긴 머리 우아하게 차 속을 흔들면
폴 폴 날리는 우매한 먼지는 언제
누구 가슴속의 기둥뿌리를 뽑을지

플라스틱 오염에 거북이도 죽고
화학섬유가 뿜어낸 미세 입자는
몸속에 박혀 치명상을 입히누면

네 코앞에 양말을 휙 벗어 던진
잘생겨도 그런 아이는 멀리하게
먼지 보듯 뻔하지 않겠나!

자연의 섭리인 지구온난화에
호들갑으로 대들 일이 아닌걸
간추린 마음에 티 나지 않게
배려의 근본이 환경 열쇠인데
아찔한 창 높이 이불을 터네

068. 파이의 가르침

지름 곱하기 파이로 둘레는 두루뭉술
맛있는 호박파이도 아닌
생각의 답에 파이는 우주 공간상인데

굽은 선의 안팎을 어떤 자로 재나
머리 아닌 발로 둘레를 뛰어 보니
딱 떨어지는 그 한 바퀴의 원주율

달리다 보면 입이 마르다가도
한 바퀴 더 달려 솟아나는 침
마흔여덟 번을 씹는 소화력에
구르는 침과 코흘리개 코가 충치를
침을 모아 삼키면 당뇨도 멀어지고
굶으면 사라지는 웬만한 속앓이에
살갗은 핥아서 낫고 마는 자연치유

너 자신을 알라는
어림에 묻은 난이의 삼박자 원기
파헤침에 끝 묻힐 윤회의 파이가
몸과 마음을 살피라는 가르침에
묘명한 새벽을 열심히 걷어내네

069. 떡갈나무

뽕나무가 뽕 뀌자
대나무가 대끼놈 하니
참나무가 참으라 했다는데

맛있는 뽕잎만 먹는 누에가 명주실 뽑느라 힘주었겠지
뼈 생성을 돕는 레스베라트롤의 오디가 먹고 싶어지네

꼿꼿이 빈 허리에 무기도 악기도 푸른 득도의 죽죽 대
봄날에 말뚝 같은 죽순이 번뇌와 고혈압을 다스린다네

푸른 강산에 참나무요 떡을 찔 때는 떡갈나무잎
도토리묵 묵사발에 아콘산이 중금속을 배출하지

참고 깨달아 멀리 보면 쓸 곳 많은 참나무인데
진작 예제서 참숯 되는 분신이 안타까울 뿐
참기도 잘도 참는 참나무 떡갈나무야
활활 잉걸불에 흩날리는 눈꽃이 소용돌이치누나

멀리 사는 이 셋이 언제 같이 모였을까
각궁에 소뿔 힘줄 뽕나무 대나무 참나무가 쓰였다니
즐겁게 모인 김에 힘껏 활을 당겨보세
흥부의 박씨를 문 봉황이 잡힐레라

070. 동지팥죽

『그놈의 소상 그래도
 뱃가죽은 얇아도
 동지팥죽은 잘 처묵네』

두리상에 둘러앉아 팥죽 큰 사발에
흥겹게 읊조려보던 가락이 있었네

배고픈 시절의 동짓날 동지팥죽
큰 그릇을 말리는 은근한 누름에도
한 살을 더 먹는 엄동설한의 맛은
뱃가죽이 얇은 아이 기다리던 팥죽
식어 빠진 팥죽이라도 맛만 좋았네

동짓날엔 대문간에 붉은 황토를 뿌리고
사발 가득 팥죽을 떠서 장독 위에 얹고
나쁜 기운 물리느라 엄마는 힘들었지
독소도 귀신도 몰아내는 우리 집 팥죽

열심히 일했으니 면역력도 올릴 겸
동지팥죽 한 그릇 맛있게 먹어보세

아랫배가 두둑해야 사장이 된다지만
뚱뚱한 내장지방도 부기도 사라지고
항산화에 노화 방지에 염증 제거로
팥죽 좋아하던 이 늙어도 날씬 빠꿈

*소상: 자식새끼, 손, 자기가 낳은 아들이나 딸
*빠꿈: 총명, 빠꼼의 센말

071. 달리기

달그림자 미소가 구르는 홀로 운동장에
발목을 돌리고 달리기 숨으로 발을 들면
가로등에 얽혀 경계에 선 나무 그림자는
학사모 십자가 다이아몬드를 만들어내고
때로는 샛별이 알듯 들릴 듯 속삭이는데
이마의 땀방울이 가슴을 적실 즈음이면
숨소리 따라 연기 피는 돌연변이 망상도
한 발 두 발 걸음 속에 어슴푸레 걷히고
달콤한 바람 한 조각이 수박같이 스친다

해님이 기지개 켜며 눈 비비는 동산에는
참새가 물고간 보석 나누는 소리 떠들썩
몇 바퀴를 뛰었나 세어보는 몸은 가빠도
시큰한 무릎 문제에는 뜀질이 보약이라
여남은 개의 턱걸이로 뻐근한 마무리에
뒷사람 생각에 버려진 물병을 치워두고
힘들어 상쾌한 새벽 달리기의 자신감은
손기정 남승룡의 올림픽을 달리게 한다

072. 망각을 넘어서

잊어버리면 떠날 수 있다
그냥

고향을 잊어버리면
낯선 감각도 없이 떠돌겠고
사랑을 잊어버리면
미련에 잠기지 않아도 되고
삶을 잊어버리면
죽을 걱정 없이
남모르는 홀로의 길 밖에야

억울탄 무리도 약 요양은 싫네
누가 따뜻한 손을 가졌을꼬

철벅 철벅 망각이
비구름을 휘몰아 머릴 두드리면
온몸이 물초가 되는 소나기에도
풀포기는 숫접게 서 있어

그래
망각을 넘어서자

* 癡呆 예방과 치료
이른 아침 찬물에 발을 씻고 合谷·太衝을 자극하며
動運動 靜中動運動 靜運動의 治癒法을 실천해보리

073. 명당을 찾아서

청개구리 우는 사연에 물길 돌리는 개울
조선 풍수 오백 년에 빼앗긴 나라 땅 땅
위정자를 만든다고 헐떡거리는 묘 터 산
어디까지 왔나. 산산이 멀었다. 다 왔다.
텅 빈 명당을 찾았는가?

잡초가 무성하면 고인 물이 많고
바짝 말라 헐벗은 땅이 길지라네

법이 평등하듯 대지는 평화롭고
지은 죄로 가는 영의 갈림길에도
흙은 몸을 똑같이 받아들이는데

얽히고설킨 방사선에 부적이나 덕지덕지
법관 의사 지관 집단이기주의 풍수 골목
이 내 몸 묻고 가야 할 텐데 걱정이로세

배산임수라
지혜 대가리 곧은 척추 반듯한 오장육부
자신을 아는 길은 생긴 몸체를 알아차림

고운 마음에 가는 정은 인지상정이요
어진 마음 잘 다스려 돕는 성정이
가슴 한곳에 뿌듯이 자리 잡는 터
이름하여 불로장생의 건강 명당이라네

이건 천기누설인데
심뽀에 명당이 묻혔다네 돈다발처럼

074. 비기지욕(肥己之慾)

내려놓거나 비우려 말게 그 마음
쓰레받기도 없고 혹 발에 묻을라

어디 즐겁고 맛있는 거 더 없나
한없는 욕심에 두루 훑어본 세상
실컷 채워봐야 간에 기별도 안 가네

내 다 가져야 그 마음 놓을 자리 비겠지
해서 채울 테니 부지런히 비우려무나
비워야 뜰지 채워야 날지 침묵의 우주선

차분히 숨 고르면 온갖 망상이 나부끼고
죽음에서 삶으로 번뇌는 회오리치다
미간에 잠자리처럼 내려앉는 물음표

비우려 애쓰지 마라
비울 수 없는 그 마음에
비움의 욕심이 안개 차면
어쩌나
비감한 비기지욕을
비움도 비우는 무이에

삶이 곧 수행이라며
어머니 강
갠지스는 흐른다

* 무이(無二): 둘이 없음, 적멸마저 비움

075. 참새 날다

동녘이 말그레 해쑥 돋으면
두 발 당겨 앉아 숨 편히 간추리고
주마등의 멋진 그림자 하날 떼어
헤아려 피우는 소람의 꽃이

감미로운 로마의 휴일
작별마저 싱그러운 사랑을
사랑을 넘을 수 있을진대

고개를 갸우뚱뚱
하지만
용마루 위 힘 맑은 참새는 알지
금방 박차고 오르는 맛을

아침마다 이리
빈 가슴에 곧은 기운 뿌듯 담고는
거리낌 없이
포르륵 초르륵 이룸숲으로

076. 십진법

"할아버지, 귤 드실래요?"
"응, 한 두서너 개만 가져오렴."
손자가 열 개나 가져왔다
"너무 많다."
"모두 합치면 열 개잖아요."
고놈 참!

"번호붙여익 가!"
"한
　둘
　셋
　넷
　하나뚤 셋 넷, 하나뚤 셋 넷."

동남 서북 한 바퀴 둥근 땅
열이 되어 열리고
넷까지만 모으니 열이 되는걸

먹구름에 햇살 나듯
하안참 뒤에야
알았네

077. 칼로 물 베기

칼로 물 베기라며
자꾸 부부싸움을 하다가는
이혼서류에 도장을 찍는다네

세숫대야에 담긴 물을 갈라보게
온전한 그릇에 금도 가려니와
시퍼런 눈을 뜨고 노려본다네

쉽다고 어설피 휘두르지 말게
물은 모든 것을 기억하고 있다네
그냥 해치겠나 접시에 담긴 물이

하하 거울을 든 저 물을 보게
번쩍이는 보검을 품고 있어
번개같이 사태를 파악한다네

상선약수를 많이도 찾지만
날 선 칼같이 행하지 못한다면
말이나 물이나 다 부질없지

사람 살려내는 칼질을 하고
맑은 물로 마무리하는데
물의 가슴에 비수를 품을 리야

078. 흡연 부스

황사 잔뜩한 거리에 이연치연으로
남녀노소 뒤죽박죽 흡연 부스에는
자욱한 연기가 무념무상 피어난다

피우는 즐거움 홀대한다며
예절도 건강도 오리무중에
미지근 봄날은 타오르다가
진달래꽃 지듯 사라져가고

아이와 약속도 거친 알림에도
참을 수 없는 것을 참는 것이
작심삼일 힘든 오십보백보

밀치듯 세워둔 고립공간으로
힐금힐금 동물원 구경거리에
아직 고뇌의 마른 속 달랠 길 없는
숨죽여 피해 가는 혼돈의 도시에는

쉰들러 리스트 고독의 가스실에
죄 없는 아우성의 역사가 스친다

079. 포옹을 기다리며

초라한 저항의 사무치는 몸부림에
불타는 지옥으로 허우적대다가
용광로에는 하얀 나비만 나부끼고

까끌까끌 청보리 성난 이삭이
사각사각 마음을 갉아 흔들어
따가운 영혼은 목메어 주저앉았다

안다미 누명은 사방을 막아서고
기적은 하늘 아련히 멀어지는데
한순간에 벌어지는 어제의 동무

말 다물고 산으로 가버린 침묵과
딱지 밑에 고스란히 버틴 상처는
멍청한 얼굴로 우울하게 서 있고

골병이 아귀 넝쿨에 감겨들어도
외래어 같은 포옹의 쪽빛 향기는
저만치에서 무늬만 철썩거리는데

뉘엿뉘엿 고난 생애 저물어가고
슬금슬금 아픈 흔적 아물어가도
간절함을 비껴가던 안타까운 날에

080. 백발 예찬

젊음을 아랑곳하지 않는 백발이
물들여 나잇값 하려는 흑발보다
얼마나 건강해 보이지 않겠느냐

벌떡 양보하는 군자가 더러 있더라도
연약한 아이 자리에 눈 흘기지 말고
아직 청춘이라는 싱싱한 그 마음으로
임산부를 앉히면 기분이나 뿌듯하지

차를 버린 탓은 미아국회나 혼내야지
어렵잖게 지혜의 장벽 넘을 수 있네
짐스럽고 힘들어도 올바로 선 몸으로

죽어보지 아니하고 죽음을 안달 수야
불길같이 다가서는 백발의 새해 넘어
내가 앞서 달려가면 희망이 솟아나련

면도기가 살을 뜯는 늙은 아침에
쓰라린 가슴은 세월 너머 잊어두고
거울 속 허연 머리에 겨울은 씨익

머리 밑동 거무레 고슴도치 함함하면
족두리에 가마 타는 옛길을 호위하며
지름길의 백발에도 백마를 달리고파

알차게 여물어 모두 즐겨 쉬는 날은
작년의 대가리를 온인하게 가다듬어
흠모하는 백발로 정갈하게 나부끼세

081. 비 오는 날

쏟아져 그리운 비가 온다
별똥별처럼 사라진 인연이
빗방울 되어 흩어 내리면
떨어져 앉은 바다의 섬들은
돌아앉아 홀로 젖어가고
추억이 간지러운 대지에는
물보라 뿌연 고독이 어린다

비 오는 날의 물청소로
쓰리게 묻은 시커먼 기억 조각
백 년쯤 됨직한 때를 걷어내고
그래도 쌓인 미련은
주룩주룩 청승에 쏟아버리고
텅 빈 마음에 한없이
그리운 비가 와서 그립다

우산도 받지 않고
비에 젖는 진달래
그리워 그리움에 풀이 죽어도
알다가도 모를 정은
솔잎에 찔린 따가움도 모른 체
봄이 다 가도록 내내
빗속의 그리움을 품어 앓는다

082. 별난 성격

'부시직' 밥 먹다가 씹은 돌
'에이' 국에 든 이 머리카락

비닐 부스러기도 뛰어들어
커피 맛이 떨떠름해요

어찌 내게만 이런 게
성질이 별나서 그렇다고

잘해주려 신경 썼는데도
설쳐대는 눈먼 유령에
한숨이 에워싼 그대 마음

조개를 씹다가 '딱'
뱉어보니 진주가 들었네
웃픈 입을 가리고 아파

계륵의 진주는 서랍 속에
성질은 저물어 치마 속에
하얀 티끌로 스미어 진다

083. 눈 오는 숲속

눈이 옵니다
하얀 소문 걸러 품고
조각조각 쏟아집니다

가지마다 가득 부딪혀
힘들게 견딘 사연들이
불꽃 웃음을 감추고 맴돕니다

하얀 숨소리 멍이 들어도
한 바퀴 세상을 춤추다가
진실의 흔적으로 스며듭니다

추억을 좇는 좁다란 오솔길
그늘 짙은 숲속에는
못 이룬 시름 사이로
알 수 없이 적시는 눈시울에
펄펄 옛적을 나부낍니다

눈이 옵니다
한세상 안쓰러워도
하얀 눈은 하얗게
한 오백 년 내렸으면 좋겠습니다

아늑한 눈밭에 팔 벌리고 누워
하얀 꿈이 걸린 줄기를 당기면
분노의 허물을 포근히 덮어주는
숲속에는
결백한 외침이 만발입니다

084. 참 풍경

새 중의 새 참새
방앗간 포수나 허수아비도 자고
포장마차에 참새구이는 없어도
뱃살 근심은 참새 물 먹듯 해야

꽃 중의 꽃 참꽃
새봄에 꽃피는 희망의 진달래
전 떡 위에 얹어 시름을 달래고
시상에 잠겨 불태운 청춘 그대

나무는 참나무 참 쓸모도 많아
다람쥐가 시샘하는 도토리묵에
한잔 막걸리 척 걸쳐 기분 내고

기름은 참기름 참나물에 참깨
참기름에 밥 비벼 한 그릇 뚝딱
고소한 영양에 병마도 물러가네

마음은 올곧은 그대의 참마음
진실에 닿으면 옥구슬이 굴러도
으뜸 자리에 참마음만 있다면야

거짓과 요설이 자취를 감추고
참머루 참다래 송이송이 맺혀
참끗한 햇살로 영그는 아침에
참 풍경 좋은 우리의 참 세상

085. 째깍째깍

시를 앞서려 초를 다투며
롤렉스와 오메가 쳇바퀴에는
서로 잘난 팔을 휘젓는 사이로
짧은 세월 더 급히 버티어 가고

허둥지둥 촌음은 잘도 달리는데
안절부절 삼추는 더디기만 하네

빨리 가려면 혼자서 가도
먼 길은 같이 가얀다지만

뉘에게 기쁨이 되는 슬픔과
뉘에게 슬픔이 되는 기쁨이
불꽃 튀는 경쟁리에

모래시계 까끌까끌
목 잡고 넘기는 아픈 순간이
죽음은 지 알아 하게 잊어두고
운명의 시곗바늘만 넘나드는데

벗어둔 흐름의 색다른 시각에
기적은 생각을 바꾸는 것이라
몸부림치던 파문은 깨쳐 들고

세월 몰래 시절을 앞서가고파
째깍째깍 앞다투어 부추긴 연
해맑은 발걸음도 이내 쫓기어
속절없는 환상을 연모해 타네

086. 마이동풍

뻐끔뻐끔 타포니가 기이키도 하여
누군가하고 숫마이봉 쳐다보니
아직 한참을 더 살아야겠느니
뾰족 돌탑 잣대의 따끔한 대웅전

오목한 구덩이는 언제나 편안하여
소복소복 눈송이 새알처럼 담기고
포근히 감싸 안는 암마이에
무덤덤 숫마이 재는 헛기침

부질없이 나불대는 어지러움이
좌우 귀때기 암수로 갈라 세워
내 편이 더 잘났다 흔들어대도

지그시 감고 녹아든 말간에는
간사한 세파에 귀 간지럽다고
한 마리 적토마 발을 내딛는데

동녘 바람 한 줄기 대한에 일면
죽순은 한 뿌리에서 쑥 자라나
앞으로 제도하는 염원의 불바람
허튼소리 이 저것 들을 새 없이
오로지 달음질치는 충절의 필마

087. 걸림돌 디딤돌

부모는 걸림돌이 안 되길 빌고
아들은 디딤돌이 안 된다 울고
시간의 약이 서로 다른 입맛에
지혜 찾아 구르는 기로의 도태

일곱 번이나 걸어 넘긴 돌부리에
여덟 번을 사뿐히 세운 디딤돌은
마음 따라 어루만진 바위인 것을

걸림돌을 손질해 디딤돌로 놓으면
행복한 걸음걸음 마루에 오르듯이
걸리적거린 삼팔선도 얼른 거두어
아름다운 꽃으로 민족을 피워야지

피멍이 들도록 가로막은 심연에서
뱀뱀이 겨를의 징검다리를 디디고
무리의 걸림돌은 디딤돌이 되었네

지겟작대기가 받쳐주고 일으키듯
이 세상 모든 걸림돌을 부둥키고
디딤돌로 일구어내는 나의 스승은
다정한 품속에서 꽃망울을 다듬네

088. 하늘과 땅과 꽃

빨간 꽃잎에 힘찬 역동
노란 꽃잎에 참된 천진
꽃잎 하나에 마음 하나
오간 정이 삼천 석인데

하늘땅 맺은 언약 잊지 않으려
철석같이 지켜 온 사랑의 계절

검고 누른 천지에 무슨 조화로
천사 나래에 고운 물감을 들여
순수 위의 고혹한 가지가지 꽃

긴 꽃대 다부지게 땅을 디디고
깬 꽃잎 너볏하게 하늘을 담고
수많은 간절 모아 맺힌 심금에
활짝 펼쳐 아름다운 열흘의 꿈

사연 없는 한 잎이 있을까마는
간직해온 속내 채 맺지 못하고
눈물도 마르기 전 짧은 만남에
뜨겁게 피는 꽃이 나는 아프네

허공을 수놓은 혜너른 참 빛이
보듬은 설원 오롯이 일군 터에
깨알 같은 우주를 품은 꽃이여

089. 살색 크레파스

검은색은 나중에 칠하라고 하셔서
달리기하는 아이의 얼굴에 먼저
살색을 곱게 입혔습니다

몽당 크레용으로 그린 운동회 그림은
특선 표를 달고 게시판 맨 위에 앉아
놀란 가슴으로 빛났습니다

연분홍 꽃잎이 바람에 휘날리어
냇물 위에 꽃 배로 손을 흔드는
숨 막히는 모습을 되돌아봅니다

열한 살에 예순이 지나는 봄날
살색으로 칠한 얼굴들이 정겹고
눈도 없는 웃음에 숨 쉬어봅니다

그려도 그려도 그리운 얼굴들이
그릴 수 없는 아픔으로 눌리면
외로이 바람을 가르던 솔잎들로
아궁이에 불길은 너울춤입니다

방금 그린 얼굴이 꺼멓게 변해도
저만큼 아물거리는 화살을 잡고
도화지에 살색을 다시 들었습니다

어느새 살구색으로 바뀐 이름에
하늘이 무슨 색인가 바라봅니다

090. 나팔꽃

파르라니 천사 날개에
발그라니 파수를 서서
채소밭 울타리에 나팔꽃 병정은
야금솔금 고사리손을 내밀고
정겨운 남자색 아우성을 펼친다

애틋한 지난밤에 못내 접어둔
저리고 아린 마음 어루만지며
기상나팔 바지런 소매를 걷는다

별사탕 솜사탕 이슬이 맺혀
세상은 똘방 사랑은 방글
속 하얀 언어를 머금은 아침에
알펜호른보다 세련된 혼으로
격정의 진주를 또르르르 굴린다

이파리 간질이는 보슬비 뜸들 새
빛바랜 꿈 살그미 군불을 지피어
천상의 견우 알알이 청보라 핀다

091. 백자 앞에서

검소하고 순진한 백의의 황홀
전통미의 표상인 백자의 자태
천하제일 비색의 고려 상감도
시공간을 초월한 진정한 명품

가만히 다가선 꺼풀 너머로는
투혼의 얼이 가련하게 박히고
금방이라도 돌멩이가 날릴 듯
은연히 조심스레 찬탄한 자랑

골동품 도자기 오마조마 유리잔에
묻어있는 조바심이 절로 스며들어
근심에 민심이 벌어지는 마음자리

정든 마을이 부스러지잖은 다행에
소더비 경매의 아슬아슬한 안목에

소소하여도 금가지 않는 믿음으로
철기문화 단단한 애정의 테두리에
불안감을 안도와 긍정의 생각으로
삶의 가치가 편안하게 이어지기를

쏟을지도 조각날지도 겁나는 숨이
하얀 찻잔을 스치는 무게로
씹어 넘기는 감은 떫은지고

092. 푸른 오월의 하늘

오월의 푸른 하늘이 희망인 줄 알았지요
나 너 없이 두드리면 열리리라 믿었지요
자라면서 내 편이 아닌 모습을 보았지요
어려서는 보릿고개 자라서는 아리랑고개
고뇌의 고비를 넘긴 빈손 쓰려 아팠지요

초록은 동색이라 푸르니 파라니 하다가
갈피를 못 잡고 추스르기에 급급하더니
인색하기 짝이 없는 농사비를 뿌리고는
추석날 차례상만 뒷짐 지고 기다리네요

독버섯으로 피어나는 거짓에 질려
새파래진 하늘도 우울했다고 하오
말라비틀어진 들판에 무지개 멀뚱
참인지 독백인지 남모르는 속말로

그 많은 세월의 꿈이 여태 여기 뒹굴어
부박해진 어린 자국 반창고를 붙여주고
까만 밤하늘에 깜빡이는 내별을 찾아서
남루하기 그지없는 구름에 돛을 단다오

냉정하단 파랑과 편안하단 초록이 엉켜
새싹은 제법 뼈대를 갖추어 돋아나오니
묘연한 푸름보다 마음의 봄날을 열어서
씩씩하게 다가오는 모습은 예와 다르오

093. 난 아직 외제를 찾는다

미군이 나눠준 초콜릿 참 달콤했던 맛
일제라면 사족을 못 쓰던 시절 있었지

수출용과 내수용의 품질 다른 인식과
우리 것이 좋은 것이라는 고깃덩어리
외면하며 찾는 수입 김치는 줄기차고
아직 못 미치는 너 나 아픈 믿음인데

주인을 기다리는 무수한 물건 속에서
쓸 만한 것이 있나 하고 쫑긋 세우니

역사 깊은 나라의 우수한 생활용품
한번 사면 만년을 쓸 것 같은 명품
이런 것은 어쩔 수 없다 치더라도

부탄이나 핀란드의 높은 행복 지수
덴마크의 청렴도 이웃 나라 친절미
이런 좋은 것들을 알뜰하게 들여와
우리 휴대전화에 실으면 좋겠구먼

부자나라에도 없는 것이 더러 있고
어려운 나라에도 모범 사례 많으니
취사선택에 나쁜 것들은 걷어내고
저기 어디쯤 넘치는 인간미를 찾아
지구 위에 이저리 새앙쥐를 굴린다

094. 검색어

컴퓨터의 검색창에 입력해보니
모르는 것이 어찌 그리 많은지
깊숙한 뜻에 보석 같은 옛말에
이런 말이 쓰일까 싶기도 한데

황제내경에 동방의 탁월한 의술 침
주은래 임어당도 인정한 우리 한문
우리만 우리 것이 아니라는 문화에
굳이 아니라고 거드름을 피운 민족
당당하게 동북공정을 막을 수 있나

별나게 삐뚠 열등감에서 발원하여
집단이해의 충돌로 갈라지는 나라
오만 위선 거짓이 횡행하는 난장판

내부에 존재하는 만성염증이 퍼지면
미래예측의 탐색에는 이렇게 나오지
통일은커녕 세계대전으로 발화하여
잿더미로 사라지는 금수강산 되리라

뭘 찾아보려 했는지 엉뚱한 화면에
가물가물 저문 하늘이 담긴 천지는
불티 강산에 탄생하는 새로운 세상
어쩌나 검색에 없는 미증유의 말을

095. 문

열린 대문으로 기침을 했더니
눈에 쌍심지를 켜고 꼬치꼬치 묻네
양상군자가 마음 문은 닫게 했다나
돈이 드나드는 문은 빼꼼하구먼

옛날의 야단법석에 미래는 닫혀있고
열린 문은 오만에 증오만 득실 뿐어
편이 다르다고 거부하는 위선의 문
나락의 싱크홀로 떨어진 지옥의 문

껌껌한 문에 올가미를 걸어두고
밤을 걷는 사람의 밤을 울리진 말게

철통 같은 문에 이리 오너라 했더니
그리움 반기듯이 방긋이 열리는 문
꼭 닫아 두어 포근한 마음의 문

견고한 문틀에 치우치지 않는 문
이리 행복해도 되나 죄스런 복문
한오백년 뒤에나 열릴 법한 문
진실의 문은 천년이 꽃이네

열린 문 닫고 닫힌 문 열릴까 봐
'열려라 참깨'
묻히게 될 진실을 굳이 외쳐보네

096. 아이와 지우개

아이가 스케치북에 연필로 그립니다
마당 넓어 대궐 같은 집에
할아버지 할머니 엄마 아빠
동생의 오뚝한 코도 만듭니다

비뚤어진 바지를 다시 그리려고
지우개로 그림을 지웁니다
사람이 많아 보이길래
할아버지 할머니도 지웁니다
부모는 어깨너머로 그림을 봅니다

검은 자국만 남은 자리가 맺힙니다
어둠이 여명을 불러오겠지만
해가 솟아도 다시 뜨지 않는 것이
있습니다
아이는 아직 알지 못합니다

바지를 바르고 멋있게 그렸으니
사랑 손에 머리를 쓰다듬어주고
아빠는 엄마에게 웃어 보이는데
아이는 지우개를 들고 있습니다

097. 금강산

이것이 무엇이오? 옷이오
저것은 무엇이오? 잣이오
이것은 무엇이오? 갓이오

배짱으로 빌어먹고 구경 나선 김삿갓은
일만 이천 제자와 금강경 참맛을 깨쳤고

마의태자 애통한 흔적이 드리운 귀면암
구룡폭포 미륵불은 무슨 까닭에 아직도
바람 맑은 물을 씻고 있을까

고요히 스며드는 바위와 물의 이데아에
떨어지는 솔방울만큼 쓰렁해진 광음에
손가락이 달을 놓칠까 머리를 뒤척이네

꿈 지고 별 총총 사정없이 쏴대는 개골
피다 멎은 봉래에 아름다운 풍악이로되
조화의 시샘에 움츠린 그늘 사이사이로
한 술 청정비바람은 깨어나길 염원이라

뉘 어디서 왔다가 어디로 가는지
비로봉에 똑똑 드는 길 물어보니
초록 숨 고르며 숨 따라간다고 하고
삼선암은 무심결에 햇발을 내뻗치네

098. 모지라진 네모 통

사람의 미음이 모지라지면 사랑이 되듯
모서리가 닳아 마모되면 뾰족하지 않고
둥글게 원만해지는 소통의 물건이 있지

때로는 웃기도 울기도 하는 반려자요
모지라진 네모 속의 온통 지하철에는
모름지기 마모시키는 젊음과
어리석음만이 철길을 달리네

홀로 조잘거리며 모지라진 네모 통에는
하늘도 졸리운 말과
없어도 됨직한 정이
부단히 우글거린 흔적을 감추는데

모지라진 옥수수가 혀를 희롱하노라면
한 번쯤 각을 세워보려던 모서리는
질 나쁜 농담도 못 해보고 문드러지네

은하수에 펼쳐둔 와이파이망에
둥그레한 하늘나라 맞닿아오면
꼭 전해보고 싶은 사연 있었노라고
센 고비를 넘도록 벼르고 있었는데

언어의 지옥으로 어찌 끈 닿아
요동치던 메모리칩 멋쩍어지니
감성마저 포용하는 반도체가 나오기를
불감청고소원의 모래알 체에 걸어두마

우뚝한 사각형이 무리로 번듯한 단지는
네모 난 귀로 여닫는 소식이 궁금할 터
저게 무지러지면 많은 아픔이 생길레라

099. 입양

똥오줌 받아내는 코흘리개에
가족도 이웃도 아닌 색다른 아이를
폐허에 금반지 찾듯 선택했을까
버려진 아일 데려다 키우겠다는
거룩한 마음씨를 누가 심었을까

고아란 고귀한 아름다움인가 보다
친부모보다 더 잘 키운 보배 선행
아름답고 깊은 애정에
고맙다는 말을 전하네

자식이나 부모를 학대하는 돈 막에
개보다 못한 계가 수두룩한 거리에
감히 입양할 수 있겠는가 던져보아
미치지 못하는 내 수준을 위로하며

큰마음을 지닌 아름다운 나라의
축복이 쏟아져 마땅한 마음씨에
감사의 고개를 숙이다가

언제쯤일까
크리스마스를 타고 올 어디쯤
세월이 버린 홀로된 코흘리개
늙은이를 입양하는 큰 어른의
수면제 없이 돌봐줄 무량심이
조여드는 가슴을 풀어줄 날은

100. 경계에 선 명상

환한 창문 앞에는 경계에 선 내가 있다
문을 열면 이곳저곳이 눈꺼풀 차이인데

사람도 자신도 믿음도 금전도 지팡이도
부러지면 다치고 마는 안타까운 한계에
부는 바람 처량하게 문풍지를 떨어대니

의지도 비움도 버리고 머뭇대듯 와닿는
여닫고 오가고 취사와 치병의 갈림길에
스쳐 가는 것이 기억의 애처로움뿐이랴

살아 그리도 애태우더니
죽음은 그리 울어 그리움 되고 말았나

웃다가 번지는 눈물은 가득하건만
울다가 흘리는 웃음은 아득하기만
만남과 이별 사이에 믿음 하나 못 심고
영화도 삼 막도 구름도 아닌 길을 밟네

능수버들 팔을 당겨 뜨겁게 늘어지더니
강 따라 쓸리기 싫어 냇가를 맴도는 물
무엇을 잃을지도 모를 두려움의 덫에서
벗어나는 으뜸 방책인 죽음을 떠올리니
아롱지는 경계에 넘실대는 초록 아우성

101. 약에 쓰는 개똥

저것이 개똥이라 말하니
똥은 오간 데 없이 내 입만 힐끗해
막상 소용되면 숨는 것이 약뿐이랴

현자는 손가락 말고 달을 보라지만
보는 달이 뭔지 알 수 없는 까닭은
가리키는 손가락만 갋네

달이나 똥이나 멀리 두고 싶더라도
추향너머 스치는 각성에
한 번쯤 마음을 건드려보고 싶잖소

지가 뭐라고
달은 개똥 품어
속박 높이 떴네

* 갋다: 참견하다, 애써 따지고 들다.

102. Ramyun broth(라면 국물)

We are all sitting around sharing ramyun, Huruluk

Love builds up as if my mouth is watering

Smells like an island and scent of golden age

The taste that everyone misses like a memory

A gluttonous old man who puts rice in ramyun soup

Despite concerns about detrimental of

a wise guy with crutches

Blup-blup water devoted to caring for ramyun boiling

Relieved from the parental burdens

Flows into the mouth or the sink

with an ironic choice of heart

The discarded broth that feels useless

Riding on my neck that keeps getting sad

Waving a pitiful light

of a nursing home in the shabby darkness

103. Silver Grass Flower(억새꽃)

I hope you work hard
Encouraged my young mind
In faded clothes and white rubber shoes
Grandpa who went beyond the sunset

Pheasants flap and play hide and seek
In the silver grass field with sparse thickets
The distant clatter of hoofs
Seems to be resurrect somewhere

Dry tears of the silver grass
that he left behind
Open the darkness
to pick up the stars

Bye
Good-bye
He's waving a white hand, but

On my feet as I turn around

Don't go
Please don't go
Incredibly thin soul
Shake it sadly

104. Goryeo Nursing Home(고려 요양장)

The hares leave to pick up plump chestnuts

The blue bird makes the blue cloth dealer cry

Even if you miss peach blossoms, apricots, and azaleas,

   The mountain valley where your dreams bloomed is gone

Mom desperately looked for her mother and

Turn the spinning wheel on the rack to the Elegy

Even if you spin it, on the spinning wheel in the air

   You're saddened by the useless days of spinning

Grandma calls her father pitifully

Even if your voice is hoarse and the night is over

Several busy children sitting with their backs turned

   There is only a faint white shadow

Fold the blanket again

Even if you find the rice you ate again

   Forty nine o'clock on a hungry morning

On a tangled road that can neither come nor go

The sky and the earth let go of their hands

  Heaven rubbed in chaos

The moon who was wiping all the sweat with a smile

She couldn't get over a layer of dirt at all

Waving her hand and closing her soul

  Goryeo sanatorium where the unfilial son sneaks in

105. My Mother(우리 엄마)

When mom's hand touches the sewing machine
The socks and the jacket came out really well
Even my gloves that were warm with colorful knitting

On the long road with a shopping bag on her head
Rubber shoes that hide sore legs
My mom is shimmer at the mirage

Our Lady, Saimdang, Empress, or Madame Curie
No matter how great they are
At my mother's feet

Even if all the stars in the Milky Way, the shooting star,
the Big Dipper, and the morning stars twinkle
They can't be like my mother who shines on me

Mom doesn't hate the wrong child
With the hot hands of sublime love
Mama smiled quietly and told me to wake up

At the end of longing

An immortal heart that grabs the moon and draws water

An infinitely proud mother is standing

In order not to get hurt or atrophy in shame

Quietly train my heart and

I have to laugh at the end

My mom sewed socks with holes in them securely

106. The first day of the last day(마지막 첫날)

Cry and it will rain for three hundred days

Even if the moon on the 17th day is distorted

When I look up, you have a bright golden face

Where the wind hung on the cliff

gasped for breath,

there were choked eyes of children who knew well

On the starting line of no return

Everything you put down is a burnt flame

In the summer when cicadas nibbling away

Rainy season, seeing you sobbing,

you must be in a lot of pain

Stepping on the rainbow bridge, the angel's meeting point

A faint smile in the fluttering clouds

The last day here is the first day there you go

The blue sorrow of a remote field

Crake

Crake

A crake is crying

107. Guelder rose(불두화)

Looking back carefully on the past sparks

When who asked what flowers I like

What flower I couldn't say

Because I didn't have a flower I liked

No matter what flower I put my heart on

Such pleasant flowers are hiding and circling

The adorable rose moss that shows off

When ten days passed, she went away

One day by the jujube tree in the front yard

Like snowflakes, like cotton candy, stretch out it's hands

In the place I always saw

The beautiful and mellow guelder rose with a white smile

It's getting dark and the night is getting deeper

What makes the white sparks dazzling

Snowflakes like big drops that stop by the window

It must be the pathetic flower of a longing mother

108. The night of Seorak(설악의 밤)

In the diligent five seasons that bloom and fade
The bitterness of the dew that accumulates on every floor
With numbness and bruising, every foot rises coldly
Lyreflowers with bated breath in cotton skirts in every valley

No one knows who dies and wakes up
After you leave, pounding on my wrinkled chest
Crossing the black mountain,
The sea at sunset hurts with sadness

Riding the clouds in the moonlight,
As a dragon twists his body and climbs up
One small but all wishes
Trace the long way to the bright star

The big rock of Daecheongbong of the rough breath
Shake his head with eyes that can't meet
You should to live a forgotten today
that will go away tomorrow
A distant shooting star draws a long line

With the dry chimney burning mind

With two hands folded sadly

I choked up and knock on the night of Seorak

There are numerous exceptions to every law

Open the way not to grieve by Heaven's command

Couldn't you come back here just once, mother!

109. An empty bucket evokes Saudade
(그리움 한 두레박)

The heartbreaking daymoon took off its white veil
The diligently running sun came to drink a sip of water
At the well where they threw buckets and chatted

Leaning on a deep dream, putting wind in the bucket
Where everything has gone to the future or the past
I'm curious about the old days, so listen carefully
It grumbles only the piled up longing

Bruised apples and fermented persimmons,
In the days when it could only be so delicious
The bucket swaying with a full breath
Summer runs away as my mother washes me the back

When it rains at the end of the waiting
The hardened ground loosens the chest and foams up
Deep eaves puddle in the dripping water beyond the podium
A colander that raises worries even if you pick up mushrooms
Even if the days of hunger healed like pomegranates

Years of hard work sweating in midsummer

Countless memories of those short but long days

A bucket of saudade that hover around plaintively

Pond skaters floating in the stream glide over cumulus clouds

The extremely dark blue leaves flutter in the hot summer

At the end of saudade, pulling the bucket string

My mother in a golden crown

110. A green leaf is falling(푸른 잎의 유영)

A longing leaf
Empty out that fresh summer day

Still so handsome green
that comforted the early summer in the shade
Even before the shadows get longer
Parting the sky with longing

The remaining leaves are fluttering
in the wild wind and rain
For some reason, leaving the white soul behind
are you fading away on the pavement

If only your breathing was a little hotter,
In the beautiful autumn leaves,
It will be boisterous with the sound of smiling pictures
Who called you so hastily?

Two crows perched on a dry branch,

They are clasping their beaks and rubbing happiness

The green leaves were supposed to be infinitely green,

but they went away without knowing the taste

How have you gone,

Mournful youth!

Did you go well?

The sad rain gradually falls on the clogged chest

111. A magpie sitting on the magnolia
(목련에 앉은 까치)

Magnolia that slept well all winter

sparkling white feathers

At the tickling whispered by the magpie

Spreads its wide arms like the sea

stretching and savoring

the scent of first love

In the neatly raised chest

The fresh green scent

Like a butterfly in the haze wave

The mountain bird holds three eggs tightly

To the pitiful grave that was drenched in dreams

Walking in the flower garden that I trimmed with my mother

The refreshing magnolia flower begins to bloom

Let go of my numb and tangled breath for a while

Around in the long sky and returning to the branch

A spring day shorter than a sigh

becomes a white lump

Over the glasses, the black plastic cries like a magpie

It seems that the magnolia is not as green as yesterday

112. Love(사랑)

Love you
Who do you admire

Love
How are you going to leave your affection behind

Make the full moon look blurry
in your clear and beautiful eyes
Skirt of bitter clouds over distant mountain

Drops of water swell in the pouring longing
One by one, the green leaves fall asleep colorfully
The red persimmons in the thorns are hot

I hope it's not a soul fire that disappears like a flame
With a long wait of fretted writhing

At the end of that longing
Hanging the string of love that melt into tears
A love that runs in search of an eternal parting

Love you
I hate you

113. Akasha(허공)

While flipping back and forth playing with my grandson
The round wall clock that move limply
It's sad to be blankly resemble the moon on the 19th

Play marbles and tipcats with quick steps in the dim memory
I flitted like a butterfly by the well of plums and cherries
In the bucket where youth and wind sleep
Only the white nights of the winter solstice were piled up

I eagerly wait for the traces that do not come after leaving
Resignation and transcendence are firmly shut their mouth
At the edge of the cliff that closes the occipital lobe
With a handful of weeds
I kept knocking on the Akasha

114. An empty vase(빈 화병)

On a purple silk base
Gently drape the green bract
Spring light rolls on the flowers
Sixteen red petals grow gracefully

A flower harmonizes
the honey-filled pistil and stamen
to create excellent elegance

The moment
I'm trying to put it in a vase

Alas
What to do
My dream ran away

115. I miss you so much(겨운 그리움)

As it's a waste to even take a picture

the camera trembled at the beautiful flower

We met on a mountain path in the morning

Barely resisted the desire to stay

I surrounded it with leaves of grass in case it gets hurt

When I came back with high expectations

To the place where I was panting and anxious

Dear me!

The broken stem bears the soul of Ichadon

Our hearts that bloomed beautifully

The relationship has become more empty and sad

than water mist

At the moist thought that lingers in my head

Even the desire to grow again is sad

The longing that is hard to keep in my heart

The sound of a flower's breath against the clear sky

116. An Old Autumn(오래된 가을)

Between the gourds entangled on the thatched roof
When the magpie flaps its tail feathers
Holding a bush broom leaning on the twig gate
Waiting for a welcome guest

The luscious brown date plum is the breast of the mother,
where the youngest dragonfly rubs her cheek
Neatly dressed persimmons in every brightly colored branch
The traveler sees the distant sky, the rainbow floats

A pine breeze creeps across the the wide floor
Flipping the pages alone, one by one
I grabbed her wrist hot that is holding the water basin
I made a promise that trembled like the first frost

A half moon dozing in a bucket full of water
The story hidden in the white hem
I am thirsty in search of scattered legends
Liquor jug covered with pine needles is bubbling

On top of the ditch where love flows

The maple leaves are rowing and the longing is lonely

The high, clear sunlight is diligently growing

Standing in the old days of a fleeting blue dream

I miss the aged autumn

117. Azalea Flower Garden(진달래 동산)

In the haze that shimmers on a sunny day

carrying a tender heart

To the azalea hill running forward like a god

Azalea flower bat made by holding hands together

Blue lips are like a mirror facing each other

Brilliant sunlight on the stone wall with my hands behind me

At the gentle whisper of a bright girl

The passing days are numb in the spring snow

A hot sunset on the azalea pink skirt

White tears puff at the end of poker

A cauldron in the reception room that used to boil fodder

The quiet old yard with scattered flames

The Azalea Flower Hill,

where the sighs of deep sorrow in the heart pass

118. Black rubber shoes(검정 고무신)

Black rubber shoes of a distant day,
shaking my head while whining that
I should only wear white rubber shoes

My grandfather smiled at the child's quibble
tapping only the brazier
with a long cigarette pipe with burning smoke

The stinging eyes looking down
I can't erase
white rubber shoes on an empty chest

Wearing black rubber shoes stubbornly
until they wear out white
I should have run through the fields

On a faded autumn day, stepping on stone steps
with dull heels and leaning against Dabotap
A crow crowing on a black roof

The days gone without realizing
Stir it's cold hands
in black burning sky

119. The First affection(첫정)

Maybe I'm a hummingbird
When I see you, my heart beats endlessly

A fresh, lively, beautiful sprout smile is
a sky full of grains
of dazzling dew on the leaves of grass

A day when I want to fly without a deer or a fairy
Even green apples in the sparse sunlight
I longed for the happiness of making a silver grass nest

Dark clouds gathered in the curved ripples
My heart sank at the echoing rumor
I didn't even know what happened to your ship that had sailed
The emptiness overlooking the winding Nakdong River
How painful it was to endure to get rid of it

The bitter soul that stood around the stone wall

could not remove the shadow of its feet

I'm afraid I'll hate the traces in the dim alley

When I stopped breathing and looked back

The years that were shabbily hidden in the heavy rain

On the chest of a hummingbird that deeply embraces the fountain

The First love is still thirsty

The sparkling green scent is rippling endlessly

120. Beauty pine trees along the Songhwa River
(송화강변 미인송)

The Songhua River runs roaringly with full waves,

The high blue flags lined up in the yard

The shouts of Balhae resounding in preparation for conquest

With the roar of attack filled with the desire for peace

Wind through the vast continent with magnanimity

A holy heart that cares for all peoples

Mt. Baekdu, that has opened its eyes wide

by controlling a thousand years

Hold high the sword that you have carefully prepared

A big dream with high aim comes true in the field

At the loud and powerful trumpet sound heading north

The bright sunlight that rises up brightly

The spirit that sprouts and grows luxuriantly

In a trustworthy love in a ponytail

The gently bloomed breath rides on a cloud boat

Golden river-crossing whispers lovey-dovey

In a beautiful deep pine scent

A green hero that appears beautifully

Grabbing the blue river and running his horse

I will unfold the bright future of the nation

The tall beauty pine trees full of the Songhwa riverside

Our kingdom used to be here

121. The bond of fate(인연의 굴레)

Put it down
Do put it down
Heartbreaking relationship
Like putting down a spoon

Cut off
Cut it off
Relationship that cannot be achieved
Like cutting a rubber band

Forget it
Forget it quickly
A relationship that has gone away
Like you have dementia

Oh Lord
What have I been doing that
Such a heartbreaking relationship
Was I trying to keep it going

Still the same
To an island of regret
Sailboat in a bridle
Suffer pain from rowing

122. It's raining(비가 오는데)

In the spring rain

The green leaves are dancing and getting darker

The outstretched hand gets wet with the tickling news

The sorrow that passed over my first love after returning home

I wish it could knock on the window for a hundred days

Bead rain

Rolling the sparkling beads again and again

After showing off, quickly run to the roots

Supernatural ants go home like bullets

Flowing and flowing energy turns the hoop

However

It's a spring rain that weeps differently from one day

Who posted malicious comments on small wishes

It's bruised and sighing, drooping and falling

Even dealing with gossip without any countermeasures is spicy

Lively rain

Even if you close all the doors, with an open heart

You need to be able to engrave the sound of the pouring rain

Let the buds bloom in the raindrops on a blue day

Will the fine rain be deceived by sweet lies and cry

123. Love between you and I, Arirang
(나와 너의 사랑, 아리랑)

Love between you and I

Love between you and I

I have to hold you back

My love for you is on the verge of breaking up

『Arirang 아리랑
Arirang 아리랑
Arariyo 아라리요
Arirang gogaereul neom-eoganda
아리랑 고개를 넘어간다』

You and I, Love between you and I

You and stranger, Love between you and stranger

Something has happened that I have to hold you

Let me go through the crisis of our love

『Ari arirang 아리 아리랑
Sseuri sseurirang 쓰리 쓰리랑
Arariga nassne 아라리가 났네
Arirang gogaero nal neomgyeojuso
아리랑 고개로 날 넘겨주소』

You and I, You and I

You and stranger, You and stranger

I have to hold you back

『Ari ari 아리아리

Sseuri sseuri 쓰리쓰리

Arariyo 아라리요』

Once upon a time, there was a crisis in our love

I wish there was no dust between us

Someone was coveting our love

When will this bitter crisis pass

It's raining and heartbreaking at the crisis of ten miles

The apron blows the years away in the cold wind

You cannot live without me

Thinking of my earnest desire to hold onto you

Do not try to leave and come back to me soon

124. Thoughts trapped in sorrow
(애수에 갇힌 상념)

7 year old boy with tears in his eyes

Painted with red goldfish on paper

How sad was the tragedy of unknown cause in the fishbowl?

Worker bees crisscross pathetically on a fragrant white flower

The acacia that was cut off as a bad tree

Did the governor who fell into a honey jar didn't know?

Acacia leaves that made love through rock-paper-scissors

The station, stopped the departing train and picked up the youth

The unforgettable romantic engineer from the old days

When I ran hand in hand with a short-haired girl

That night, the black river on a midsummer night will flutter white

Grandpa calls his grandson at the floor of the Sarangbang

where summer is coming to an end

The deep weight of two bags of Pungnyeoncho to bring to mother

It's a long rainy season with dark years of cigarette smoke

from her husband who went to Seoul

If the blooming didn't come out to meet the spring

did mom leave it for so long and go far away?

Mother who does not come, who will rather wait for me now

The sun is setting at the sound of leaves gnawing away the years

Into the unknown tomorrow, Oh! Susanna, let's sing this song

You can walk comfortably

only if you firmly believe in the ax you trust

The sound of sutras brushes the ears of the ox

The eyes of cows chewing fodder are uncomfortable

125. Legacy(유산)

The seasons and years
Roll around bumpy
Cumulus and storm clouds

Grandpa grandma
Father and mother
The way all went

More stains all over the place
on the picture with a closed mouth
Sweat shed by harvesting

If you stop and look back
On a dim silk road
beautiful relationship

Can't see or hear
Can't know or catch
The day that changed and disappeared

Straight orchid in the garden

A single ray of bright purple

Finally creates a lonely exclamation

A bright face with a right mind

to a poor heritage

Bluntly

The sunlight that leaves as if to stay

126. The leaves are falling(낙엽 지는데)

Falling into the silence of an empty mind
The sound of clean rain on the rare paulownia leaves
Longing is bubbling with water drops
The faint afterglow of the love that has been dropped
pat on the shoulder

Like a sailboat leaving,
on a leaf that cuts through the darkness
It's disturbing that my heart is falling
A hesitant promise to a stone wall
Clumsy promises are forming to my chest
The cold frost of the lonely autumn that seeps through

Even if we meet again tomorrow
Sad to say goodbye today, finally
At the sound of a gray whistle hitting a dark mountain
Forgetting the promise not to be sad even if we are lonely
I made myself cry, the leaves are falling

A child who enraptured in autumn long ago
wanted to be the god Apollo
Wisdom lurks before love
The moonlight soaked in restraint from me
Go down by rowing on a paulownia leaf

127. The next(다음)

There is a first, there is a next
  Next of the next is the painful end

In the eyes with the sword
  Even the deepest heart is the sea on the plate

Even if the intertwined words and writings pour into the sky
  Throw it in the air and untie the skein

Not shaken by the wind
  Not intoxicated with the scent
    Not attracted to light
      After you make up your mind

Knock on the bright door
  Finding a way in the open sky
    See right away, know right away, go right away

The next world to come
  The next day that we don't know
    Who exists to open the next world

The refreshing sunset slowly seeps in
  A vivid and clear smile in the dawn sky
    Rolling on the pear blossoms

128. Nostalgia(향수)

Even if it passes by
I want to stay forever
Even if I casually forget and live
Sometimes the arrow-like feeling
was quickly crossing the stepping stones

A mountain bird built three eggs nest near the grave
To the garden where the curly pasqueflower bloom
Filling the spring in a bamboo basket of gathering wild herbs
Hope was rolling desirably on the golden grass

The swing with a thick braided rope hanging
from the biggest Pogu tree in town
When the swing winds into the past and into the future
At the fluttering skirt hem, we smiled dizzyingly

At the hem of grandfather who traveled a long way
The sleeping chick runs to her mother in the stable
A flock of sparrows shook the jujube tree

The riddle of "It bow down to a distant mountain"

If you hit the treadmill, there comes out

as pine rice cake and mugwort rice cake

It's broken and lumpy, the taste of stepping with my foot

The beats of turning over and pounding fit perfectly

From the time the star–like persimmon flower bloomed

it was threaded and waited

The ripe persimmon urged the basket to pick

them up quickly in angry red face

On a wedding that the whole town is full of festivity

Pierce a hole with my saliva finger and look in

I used to play the bride and bridegroom with my peers

Inside the gate where the moon thief passes

The savory taste of dinner table

filled the wide floor like puffed maize

In the neatly worn rubber shoes on the stepping stones,

White snowflakes are getting wet in search of their hometown

The bizarre old story of my aunt who couldn't get married,

was wrapped around a cotton blanket and the night became thick

Shrugging shoulders to an exciting day

Running through the road as raise a cloud of dust

In the arm of the world's cozy mother

I went to dreamland while breastfeeding on mom's arm pillow

Even if nothing is left

Everything comes alive

The longing that gathers like New Year's Day

In a cozy courtyard that's filled with emotions

I want to knead the soil to stack the broken wall

129. Grasshopper(베짱이)

A flower garden where you trim the stars with a saw
Slowly played the Geomungo on the loom rhythm
A cheerful melody that lightly rubs silk thread

In the law where there is no law
Beating the generous glimmer of darkness
The shy white petals are covered with a veil
Kung Duk Kung Duk beats my heart

If the grass bug's cry wasn't bitter,
How does the thin moon bloom again
Would I have overcome the lamentable crisis?

The world depended on the end of a wish
In the character of persevering without bending
Perfecting it diligently and straighten it out

Flowers bloom in old age due to the hardships of youth
Become a rich family and give generously
Gotta live like a grasshopper with big guts

On this night when hope blooms
In the flower garden where the starlight whispers
Made by working hard in secret
Carrying a confident back
Grasshopper guts that bounce the sky

130. Poseokjeong(포석정)

The breath of the pine trees bent on the back
of the Namsan pine forest road
The sound of drums that deeply struck a thousand years
It blooms thickly in the dazzling sunlight
Poseokjeong Pavilion with a profound feeling in a curved groove
Even if the empty years of the winding water have stopped

Able to spread the will of wealth and prosperity with the king's wine
We raised the holy cup and be polite and drink sacrificial food
Twenty-two meters of round abalone waterway historic site No.1
Glad to see Hwarangdo, Hwabaekhoe, and the land of reunification

In the beautiful faults sowed with
the seeds of diligence, self-help and cooperation
Mourning President Park's loss to crafty Cutter
Disappeared by itself while trying to erase the history of Silla
Yesterday, today and tomorrow's Big Dipper Sky,
who resolutely embraced a crowd full of hostility

On the full moon when the millennium of forgiveness swells

in the king's clothes

Floating a poem on the goblet, a traveler with deep wrinkles

Overcome hardships by offering sacrifices to the heavenly gods

Ganggangsuulae holding hands in hands and

walking around Poseokjeong under the moonlight

I'm laughing along, but he pretend not to know

131. Enigmatic World(수수께끼 세상)

What is a waterwheel without water?

It's your wheel that doesn't turn

Really?

What makes the Earth move?

It's money

You guessed it

What does the mind look like?

It's like a rough diamond

Angular pain will also disappear when it is round

What's in your aunt's pocket?

Me, what's in the pocket is me

I'm a sword rooted in money of greed and jealousy

What will the mister man believe?

His mysterious backer

His eyelids swell for fear of missing the money line

If you work hard, money will follow

Learning, broadcasting, public opinion, independence

Everyone risk their lives for money and run crookedly

We should stop going the wrong way now

Is the world going well?

In the stopped watermill, my grandson play cute tricks

My wrinkled hand hurts in my ragged silk purse

Those coming dark clouds will pour Noah's flood

The ice puzzle that will melt soon!

132. Legitimate option(선택사항)

In search of a splendid rest,

I'm going to choose the demise of a king

What kind of death has passed through the flower garden

Died and passed away at the end of his life

He went to heaven and fell asleep in Zen Buddhism

Die in harness, immortality entering nirvana

It's sad, but the life of death is only regrettable

Fill in the blanks by writing death at the corner of paper

Leaving traces that are not even tiger skin

Dispersed Requiem to Death

Just like everyone is born to their own mother

The paths we take are different

A place you don't know until you stand at Myeonggyeongdae

(A mirror at the entrance to the underworld)

Look up to heaven, talk too much to hell

I hope it's not a shameful death

so you can choose before you die

What kind of life will you want to end?

Even if you choose well, if the hearts around you turn away

It will be a UFO hover in the air and cross the mountain

Even if you go, don't worry about breathing

Like the dazzling dew on a dry leaf

You lived without lies in the blue sky

For a thousand years or so, sometimes the feelings are new

The final choice is still waiting

133. Word tastes(말맛)

Saying hello seems like someone is peeping in a hurry
I'm indisposed with dry feelings,
rather than asking if you have eaten
It's less savory than the word Banga

Costa Rica's Pura Vida
To the rich hope of a life that seems to be going well
It's relaxing as if it's raining the blue rain of happiness

Adios of Spain
Even the passing farewell is in vain
The bitter and aching taste of parting is dripping

Moai, stone statues of Easter Island
As the Mangbu-seok of Surijae in honor of her husband is weeping
It is the Mangmo-seok of mourning to commemorate the mother

If you go now, when will you come back? Oh, sad, sad.
At the foot of the mountain where
the sorrow that soothes the soul grabs the bier
Breath of red plum blossoms in the pouring snow, be cruel

Without a word, a warm affection melts my frozen heart

The true taste remains the same as it was the first time

A parrot that chirps many words in vain, nothing happens

Our deep, pathetic, eternal love

The taste of the words outside the mouth is

scattered in an instant and is vain

Until you leave, don't change, hold the words tight

*The Mangbu-seok: stone statue waiting for husband,
 a legendary faithful wife who died and was turned to stone waiting for her husband, the stone on which a faithful wife stood waiting for her husband until she perished

*A Mangmo-seok: stone statue waiting for mother,
 a legendary faithful child who died and was turned to stone waiting for his mother, the stone on which a faithful child stood waiting for his mother until he perished, I thought

134. The last minute(마지막 순간)

Even if we meet again tomorrow

The sad thing about breaking up today

'Cause the moonlight leans on the thin clouds

'Cause I couldn't pour the wine left in the empty glass

'Cause the light rain gets wet in my tender heart

'Cause I can't forget you

Maybe this moment will be the last

A thing, a person, or any last

It's still, sometimes I can't forget, I'll miss you

If it's a black day with no wind

Even the sky will be choked with unforgettable longing

The ending of the movie is so futile

The main character who left on their way

There is only an empty aftertaste in the white seagull

I climbed Mt. Biseul and looked at the Nakdong River

The river that surrounds the mountain has cloudy ends

Even if you can see it, the haze that hides it

Jujubes are ripening red

Even if you whisper the birth of a clear energy

Now in the hands of letting go of the world

How hard it is to say goodbye

It's so sad to say it's the last

Last

I hope the last moment never comes

Close my eyes quietly and pray eagerly

135. Find some numbers(수를 찾아서)

Even if the yellow envelope is thin at first
Received once a month for hard work
From one day on, my salary left only the smell
and piled up in numbers in my savings account

In my palmier days
I clumsily divided the numbers here and there
As you know, the share that is over
The circle of money keeps getting thinner

It takes a widow to know a widow's difficulties
I need to collect more considering where to distribute
In the deepening sigh of a lonely soul
I have a long way to go, but the day is setting

It's not a number, but 0 is round
Because there's a hole in the broken sky
Go on a mountain road in search of gold mines
You say it's an irrational number
Without knowing my intentions

136. Duck and drake(물수제비뜨기)

I put my backpack down by the calm river

Throwing flat stones wisely

A pretty butterfly that lightly walks on water

You six times, I just one

The joy of betting in skip stones

Give strength to the index finger holding the edge of the stone

Bend your body to the side and throw a stone with arm

In the acrobatics that flap like a goblin jumps

Thoughts and the sky fall asleep in ecstasy

Water drops twinkle white clap

The day that skip stones scattered sharply

Kicking off the unfamiliar flowing water

Saying I'm here

Somewhere where you show your clean face

Holding on to a small stone

Skip Stone's splashing water

is the most delicious today

Through the branches where the big snowflakes pause

Snow-skip stones

Green dreams come true

137. Mental civilization of change
(변화의 정신문명)

In a small house filled with the warmth of love

Enjoying a meager table in modest attire

Stay healthy by bus, subway and brisk walking

Encourage them instead of fingering in the mistakes of others

Even if you know a little bit, study harder and work harder

Lower yourself and respect the other person

Be polite and treat them without high and low alike

Don't tax evasion, be honestly thrifty

Criticize with alternatives but become a true patriot

Listen to advice, handle work with your neighbors

The fault is responsible for each other and boasts the country

Be united in what many people do

to become the most beautiful nation in the world

Even if the great man who sacrificed his life

to save the people has gone

It is our earnest hope to become such a country

In an era that calls for change, the real thing is

I have to live like this before anyone else

The mindset of making people comfortable

should be the value of social norms

138. A lonely wish(고독한 바람)

In the middle of eating
I wonder if the Creator is standing with a staff
Looking at the sky

In the dry sunset that the wild geese left
Through the gaps where the flock of clouds rest
God, who has embraced the past two thousand years,
is probably too lazy
I wish I could see you once or twice

When a creature becomes dirty, it can be washed immediately
It seems like the world is still resting and unstained
Clean it off with a broom of purification
You have to hit it hard, the universe will spinning right

Splash, a great white shark jumping over Mt. Gwanak
I put the bone on the spool and ran excitedly
In a blink of an eye, it's driving a rocket to meet someone

Where did you hide? The peek-a-boo star of the blue dream

Lonely hide-and-seek where even the clairvoyant becomes blind

A light that draws a stroke after spending time in contemplation

In spite of the independence that endured painful hardships

Where is someone to eat with

Holding a blank sheet

Longing paper

139. A class that disseminate happiness
(행복을 펼치는 수업)

People want to be happy but they don't know

what a happy life depends on

The one precious thing is to live each day without getting sick

They think of putting their sick body to an unknown hospital later

No one tried to connect the childhood dream of becoming a doctor

Children in doctors gowns holding stethoscope and

opening first aid kit playing in hospital

Grandma touching my tummy with healing hands

There is the ability to cure incurable diseases even in shamanism

There is no doctor who knows his body as well as he does

Laying the foundation for learning one or more medical

techniques from elementary school

So that everyone can become a doctor who takes care of diseases

We can help children develop their playing house therapy talents

Universities make it a compulsory subject, and on the day that
all people become doctors
The pain in my heart disappears with the warmth
of my daughter who says 'ho'
To prevent the epidemic from getting too far, to save yourself
Humanity, wouldn't it be appropriate to implement national
medical education from an early age?

Educate students to develop correct sexual knowledge
Prevent misdiagnosis, tyranny, group selfishness
and leakage of medical expenses
To get a job other than the basic job of a doctor
So that no one gets sick and everyone gets rich!

140. Adoption(입양)

In the little kids that dispose poo and pee
A different child who is neither family nor neighbor
Choose them as if you were looking for a gold ring in the ruins
Who planted the holy heart of raising someone else's child

An orphan is a noble beauty
The good deed that raised them better than their real parents
I hope to show my gratitude for the deep affection

For money that abuses children or parents
On a street full of systems that are inferior to dogs
Do you dare to adopt
Comforting my level that I can't reach

In a beautiful country with a big heart
In a heart that deserves blessings
I happily bowed my head

Then, When will it happen
Somewhere that seems to ride on Christmas
A lone adult kid that has been abandoned by time
Infinite mind to caring for you without sleeping pills
When will the day come when a grown-up
who adopts an old man will release my tight chest

218

141. Such a beautiful scenery(참 풍경)

The real bird among birds is the sparrow
The mill, the hunter, and the scarecrow are gone
Even if there is no roasted sparrow at cart bar
Drink like a sparrow to get rid of belly fat worries

Among the flowers, the true flower is the azalea
Azaleas of hope blooming in the new spring
I put it on top of the rice cake to relieve the pain
You, who burned your youth in the idea of poetry

The true tree, the oak tree is very useful
In the acorn cake that the squirrel is jealous of
Put on a cup of makgeolli and feel good

The true oil, Oil is sesame oil and sesame seeds
Mix rice with sesame oil and enjoy a bowl
Even sickness recedes due to the delicious nutrition

The true heart, Your true heart is quiet
Even if the jade ball rolls when it touches the truth
If there is only true heart in the highest position

Lies and rumors have disappeared
Muscadine and Siberian gooseberry are forming in clusters
In the morning ripening with the true sunlight
Our true world with beautiful scenery

142. Is it polite country?(예의 바른 나라라)

I'll ask you one

Do you think you are polite, so are others polite

If so, would Confucius have said any words of courtesy

Then what courtesy can you say

Everyone is delusional with no manners

Being crooked in politics, clubs, or corners

Forgive it and you feel betrayed

Then what courtesy can you ask for?

Like father, like tainted son

Even if you pretend to be good in a bright place

Doing all kinds of bad things in a dark place

Keep your head down when you are greedy for money and power

It is common not to repay borrowed money

A social atmosphere that exploits and steals the wealth of others

When Confucius saw the young eat meat and the old bones,

He was trying to lead them to a polite country in Goryeojang

Interpret it to our advantage, A country with no manners

If you did it knowingly, it would be more crooked
If you didn't know, fix it right now

It's embarrassing for foreigners to know the truth
It's weird when they ask me what manners are
Even if I say it with a shy face, we should know

The lamp of the East is tilted and dim
Wouldn't it be so easy to make a courtesy country!

143. The coffer surrounded by conspiracy
(음모에 둘린 궤)

The turtledove that picked up the words in daylight

Donkey King's Ears Locked in Seven Hours

Shaking it's head and crying nine times

Will the black rat who stole the words in the night

confess in front of a stray cat?

The story of the princess's wounded coffer

In the frame of a thief plotted by an evil group

Charge her with a fault

that made a mountain out of a molehill

Few are on the right track

In the fire of a goblin shaken by slander

Come this way, go that way

A flock of hungry carp follows empty-handed,

chasing and chatting

A tempting ear trapped in a rake of intrigue

Between the split eyes and the chest

The devil's tusks that smash the mist

Even if a walking bull wields its long tail

Unable to eradicate mosquito bites by secret collusion

If you know the true meaning of living together

Everyone who is conscious gets up

Open the coffer surrounded by darkness

The princess puts on a gold ring

Put two silver bracelets on the conspiracy

144. The cuckoo(뻐꾸기)

Quickly push the eggs into the Korean crow-tits' nest, cuckoo
In the flycatcher's nest, the cuckoo lays its eggs, cuckoo
I don't know you, sit back with a straight face, cuckoo
On a suffocating and burning spring day, cuckoo

If we take out the rubber tube that sucks up maple tree water
Will the hyenas move the the national treasury back to its place
Sitting on top of the money for the grieving victims
Holding weight as if righteously, blood-sucks parasite, cuckoo

In a crooked world, you have to live by deceiving
In the truth that has been covered, buried and overlaid
Instead of thanking me for raising it well, You're upset
The guy who farted gets angry, gloomy cuckoo

Stupid thief trying to rule by pretending to serve
Saying in that hubby that guy, gets mad at us for no reason
Strangely enough, they kept chiming in blinking, cuckoo
Even without genetic testing, goldfish are blinking

The cross cuckoo and vomits red blood
Yellow sailboat is torn black by the offerings
If you don't innovate, will the right day come?
When do real flowers bloom?
A pitiful cuckoo cries in a barley field, cuckoo

145. Beautiful smiling teeth(여소치)

If your smiling teeth look genuine

That the world is still very foolish

The white darkness will laugh black

Ridicule and slander with the curse

Unlike the inside, look around is a trap for Yeosochi

Don't think all smiling girls are pretty

Don't think all smiling men are kind

Show a stranger the wrong way

The road I passed without knowing it was in vain

I really don't know the teeth that smile beautifully

The warped angel is like that

Reports of espionage have gone nowhere

Mistakes caused are pinched like lightning

A strange smile wet in the spring rain

Yeosochi mocking the distorted sky

Showing teeth and smiling

Confused at the smiling face, I swallowed my saliva

Over the unknown face of a sword hidden in laughter

How many people know that they don't know

146. Stainless steel(스테인리스스틸)

Stainless steel that does not rust will also rust

The gold in 99.99% is called pure gold

Permanent things are not semi-permanent

When it breaks down, becomes irreparable garbage

The percentage of ingredients marked as 100% is unclear

A person's life is only a hundred years old

Destiny says it's ninety-nine, and he cuts one year off

The president who cried for great unity

became a milestone for division

His words, sworn firmly, are snaking around the issue

The people are annoyed by the sin of not making a good country

You're the one who makes fun of the person who chose you

The egret turns around in hidden clothes

White on the outside and black on the inside,

all over the place turning gray

Crying love, swallowing it with treachery and throwing it away

Even if the considerable age world tries to act his age

Waves colored with greed come crashing down into rollers

Caring is tied to a red light across the road

A forked tongue will be bound together or split into three?

I beat the rust-free brass with a yardstick

Everyone who has gone is endlessly saddened by the truth

Pass the years of not commenting on the truth diligently

Responsibilities and restrictions are the belly button to enjoy freedom

Drops of water dripping from a tightly locked faucet

are a boiling bonus of wasted life

147. Power pole(전봇대)

Stood tall power pole at the entrance to see the distant mountain

The jolly black dog raised his hind legs and grinned

The boy who came staggered and hugged it warmly

and then trembled and never says goodbye

The bald gentleman threw an old bag away

Shaking his empty hands, he glances at the sky

Will it rain or thunder

A large luggage bag provided by a woman driving a car

A long-haired woman with a nice glove and a black mask

sticks a piece of square paper and trotted

A sudden kick of a young guy approaching from somewhere

might not be the expert

On a cloudy day in the rainy season

Power pole is thinning with a buzzing sigh

Even the fleeting leaves add a dream of comfort

On the way to become a white powder butterfly
scraped off by a bunch of shoulder straps
Would a congressman with a handsome face
sang a congratulatory song?

A new city that is once again shoveling redevelopment
Winding around a long power pole without guilt
In the season of being buried by the wind like a blade
Mountains criticize short power pole

148. The gulf(격차)

A shillion won by picking up a blank sheet of paper

It's made of platinum

I'll write a nice wedding proposal

If you ruin it, just throw it away

If you try to give, no one will receive it,

but if you throw it away, it disappears quickly

They say he bought it with an eye to recognizing its value

Ten million won for a luxury handkerchief

Can it be good that parting is expensive

I'll just wipe my tears and throw it away

It will go to the sick country

Organic apples cost thirty million won each

If it's for you, this is nothing

Farmers should also be treated

You don't even know that it's rotten, or you don't

If you look closely, you will know, but someone who knows

This house is only worth a few trillion won

If it rains, I have to push it away and build it again

This is a house where my family will live,

so we have to build it well and live a long time

Of the fund man who was devastated by the collapsed pillar

Where are the waitresses and security guards

I am relieved that the gap between rich and poor was a dream

I can still buy water and ramen for only one thousand won

I bought five for only one hundred won, so I'm very rich

149. An apartment(아파트)

The apartment is wriggling in pain
My head is pounding and my heart is heavy

The missing matchboxes seem to be all piled up here
High-rise buildings and fear of heights
In a speculation that goes beyond value and salary
We grumble at the right to sunlight, view, and extortion taxes
It's moldy, it's leaking, and it's noisy
It's a crazy house built by someone else

Even if it's not Corinthian or Renaissance
A home should taste like a comfortable life
who lives in that sick apartment
Both common sense and the gates of order are at risk
I can't even buy a common Gangnam apartment
Boy, I'm stinging at the sound of resentment

Redevelopment that makes the land cry

Reducing the lifespan by stating its useful life

At the feet of a rich bear selling information quickly

An upset dog can't even look at the roof

Rusty steps in a disposable apartment

Full of painful values and lingering feelings

Chimney of a thatched house where potatoes are boiled

I guess I can't sleep for a long time because

I've been burning so many shabby dreams

150. Dragon Dream Trap(용꿈의 함정)

Don't dream of dragons

Even if there was a dragon, the animal that disappeared

The dragon was the plaything of the scoundrels

Are you going to die of anger, no matter how lucky you are

The dragon is a plausible imaginary

Six dragons appeared and made fun of Yeouiju

It was created to win people's hearts

In the days of dreams, everyone tried to be a dragon

Don't dream of Phoenices

Even if there was a phoenix, you won't be able to see it anymore

Phoenix was made to deceive women

Don't be a phoenix, don't even hold a phoenix

I wonder if a precious thing that seems to be good is really good

The smell of chicks on the skirt is weak

Stop knocking on the window while sleeping

The swallow spurs up the water, is prettier than phoenix

If an earthworm is a dragon and a chicken is a phoenix,

Old palace that can't stop you from doing so

On a muggy day, have a bowl of dragon and phoenix soup

A night I dream of a dragon and want to buy a lottery ticket

If you can control your dreams, your mind is clear

Hope to get to the gateway, spread it out on the desk

To wander fearlessly, with the ambition of staying under the bushes

Let's fly high in the sky with the cool struggle of the dragon

151. When I turn on the TV(TV를 켜면)

When I turn on the TV

They say goodbye and see you tomorrow

Only the oinking sounds is deafening everywhere

Guys in white gown tell you to go to the hospital if you're sick

In vain efforts to change channels against loud advertisements

The rain forecast that is not in the sky resembles a country

Grabbing the cloud's tail and waving tomorrow

The sound of people and singing is strange on their lips

A sharp instrument swallows the voice and burns my ears

Hard sounds would have sat crying on art and meditation

To the announcer who twists the partial facts

The divided panel is in the sophistry of forgetting ghosts

In a play where you sit on the far left and fight to the end

Even the weeds become dull in the arguing

In a beautiful voice that has been purified without frills

When is the true delivery of unjudgmented facts?

I can only hear dogs barking in the square box

shouting evil for money

I'm gonna save on electricity bills

The screen is torn because it hurts

I can't put it on as a band-aid anyway

A million dollars is wasted in a few days

So, I turn off the TV

152. The components of the zoo
(동물원의 구성요소)

Sitting with a hammer without right path

A referee who only knows the way he knows

without field investigation

Present the fallacy of clumsy standards

Hits the goblin's bat. Boom boom

A strange force turns its head, closes its eyes and knocks

Abandoning common sense and without virtue

The goblin bat mumbles that

only one side is my animal

For my convenient taste, in a fickle policy

Tomorrow we can tear it apart again

The congressmen chosen by animals, who knows?

I like how good the bat is in the match

The goblin bats that chime in with each other 'go-man-go'

Even the arrogant zoo is a mirror in my hand

The goblin's bat follows mindlessly

Three bats are running like crazy

Turd, come out. Click clack, click clack.

I don't know, Click clack, click clack.

Holding hands and arms with a clean heart

Zoo components in my hand

Goblin, go away. Get me some gold!

Heavenly peaches will fruit in our cage

153. Antiques(골동품)

Do you ignore him because he is old fashioned
Don't be funny
He has an enlightened smile already

With power falling into exclusive individual heroism
Do not unreasonably treat the rights and interests
of the elderly without even asking the old man
It won't be long before you realize it

I'm not standing still because I'm a straw bag
It's ridiculous, but it's a glimmer of hope

There are some houses
that do not treat one old and rare household item
as a dull item that loses the sense of the times
and serve them better than their parents

To the prosperity of a straight-forward family
Who doesn't want the blue comes from indigo
Antiques only endure dizzying value
Shouldn't it just be useless because it's insignificant

154. Space of beliefs(신념의 공간)

The existence of light and wind
Even though there is no weight, press my heart
The ghost's face feel like my blood is curdling

Place a space of relaxed belief
at the bedside where I can bend my elbows
I might be swayed
at the weight that is not valuable and
on the face that hides the truth
I have to raise to the standards without generosity

In the pouring downpour of rain
Sarah typhoon is breaking
The phone ringing in the morning
It's a sign of a sad death

Like a drop of water falling on a taro leaf
Roll my head back and forth on the arm pillow
In a space of faith with old and twisted standards
Elbowroom that shrinks as time tightens
Spreads out as much freedom as a straw

155. How to stop bullets(총알을 막는 법)

Judgments take years and decisions are vague
A sentence that overturns common sense is clenched in fists
Errors interpreted by the court because the law is difficult
They don't even see the facts, they just hammer the letters

Even the courts are struggling with difficult legal texts
As there is no doctor who can cure my disease
There are countless judges who do not know the law

Make the law right so you and I can easily see
In a country where the right standards are beautiful
Let's make sure there's no one elude the law

In the north, aiming a big gun at the south
In the south, shooting language guns at each other
Before the day comes when the bullets rain
It must be firmly blocked by a bullet-blocking method
When everyone is dead, who will stand in court

Don't create statistic traps to hide
Don't say that you don't have tangible evidence
if you gain a confident belief
Don't let dogs sniffle in Lenin's trash can
Let's keep the law that doesn't go beyond common sense

156. For the crucian carp to beat the shark
(붕어가 상어를 이기려면)

For crucian carp to defeat shark

Draw in fresh water

Gather and attack

Hits important points like lightning

Pay another shark

Not good enough

Ask God for help

North Korean nuclear bomb on shark's neck

Rumor has it that fins are tonics

Yes that's fins

Natural enemies are many human beings

Why should I have known

Omigod

That's a big deal

That person who's not even Kang Tae-gong

He is harassing a crucian carp

by setting aside the shark's fin

157. Dog(개새끼)

Since becoming a human child
Even if they are all same children of the person
The name that's hard to call is dog-baby

Everything changes, so is it a dog or a person
The same immature child in the blurring sunset
Treat their parents like dogs, and dogs like children
Surfactants are also tired at the boundary

Hate builds up by inciting and harming others
Biting the hand of the owner who feeds him
Bad words and actions are criticized
Scolded the dog-bastard with a bitter cold heart

Lots of people like to eat piglet, but
Boshintang, the traditional habit of caring for others
Treatment is far from the fluctuating pandemics
A group of selfish evil dogs committing terrible sins

A dog whose leash is unleashed

Attack and runs rampant as humans are parents

Who can afford a human dog's teeth

The dog that barks at the moon hides its tail

Dogs need to stay away from people now

To a paradise on earth where no bastards run wild

Let's make Korea a shelter full of consideration

158. Corporate body(법인)

To the members of a corporation personified by law
Should you limit their lives?

They became a family after fierce competition
in a lifelong job where they worked like their masters.
If nothing goes wrong, let them work for the rest of their lives

Under the pretext of honorary retirement, or restructuring
If you cut and throw away their long lives
Are families, corporations, and society normal?

If you picked one talent,
Even if you don't know the afterlife, you have to guarantee
the time of choice that took away the hard years of old age
If he dares to leave, then you can't help but

Breaking the frame of competition, which is a shallow tactic
Change the corporate law so that people can live
Can't you make a land of morning calm?

In an embrace like the sea that accepts everything
An unwavering society of strong trust
To make tomorrow's world a better country
Shouldn't it be the right system?

Among the people who come and go to Myeongdong
Is there a mixture of two or three crying ghosts
To the lawless black hole of Cosmos Department Store
The stars with outstretched arms are being sucked in

159. Waiting for a hug(포옹을 기다리며)

In the wretched struggle of shabby resistance

Floundering to a fiery hell

Only white butterflies flutter in the furnace

The rough green barley's angry ears

Nibble and shake my heart

The stinging soul was choked and sank down

The framed accusation is blocking all sides

Miracles fade away in the sky

Yesterday's friend who becomes an enemy in an instant

The silence that shuts its mouth and goes to the mountain

The wound that remained intact under the scab

Standing depressed with a stupid face

Even if a severe disease is wound around the vines

The indigo scent of hugs like a foreign word

Across the street, only the appearance is waving

A life of hardship is coming to an end

Even if the traces of pain slowly heal

On a sad day when you evaded my earnestness

160. Millstone and crow(맷돌과 까마귀)

Can't eat it because it's high, waste to give it to others
It's Magpie rice left behind by the ill-tempered poke
The tasteless persimmons left by magpies
The crows that share thriftly
With the ingenuity of filling a water bottle with stones
Tell me someone's dead house like a ghost
What a wise black devil

The salt mill that greed threw into the sea
You must be spinning around in a salty sweat today
Water and salt faded by avarice

The crow of the persimmon tree with a good feeling to love
If you take a millstone from the sea and come out
Clean salt without worrying about high blood pressure
It would be a world without worrying about drinking water

Hot and annoying days with nowhere to go
It's cool when you dab saliva on your nipples and fan them
Spreading wisdom in all the heavens
On the black wings that twinkle on the millstone
Let's plant the sensible meaning, Caw, caw!

161. Sublimate love by breathing
(사랑의 승화 호흡)

There is no point in making too many confessions

Because it's buried in the sins of the mind

From the ironic heart of wriggling desire

Let's get out of the mud like a lotus flower

When impulses come rushing in like a volcano

Breathing meditation for sexual desire control

Looking at the tip of your breathing nose

Just breathe quietly until you count to ten

With the desire to do it and the thought of refraining

It's hard to change to a breathing position, but

Before the count of three, you will feel the joy

of being released without anyone noticing

Calm down and feel your in-breath and out-breath

If you look at it without positive or negative

Enlightenment is very near and easy to achieve

If you win with your breath, your body comes alive

Freedom from sexual problems is deliverance state

Neither the monk nor the priest experienced

Transcendental sensitivity is right here

Against the guilt of suffering from poor sex education

Don't run away pretending not to be all of you

Breath that sublimates love into purity

Take a breath and shake off the pain

In lotus position, the moon rises on your forehead

and the sun rises in your clear mind

162. Cicada(매미)

Rolling around and enduring seven years
Maeng~
As the firstborn son comes into the world
As Tarzan cuts through the jungle
Clearly resonates the flawless heart

Be a much better Cicada than before, remove the white skin
Little by little, the blue lesson spreads seven days
In the space of consideration that burned the heat
The crown of five virtues is clear

On the cicada's shell facing the sky
The virtue of the cicada larva for treating
atopy, cataracts, and otitis media is sublime

A cool breeze that drips
Like flowers, cicadas, or dewdrops
Even if you pick up the traces of a short life
Mem, mem, mem, mem, Maeng~
A hero who disappears because of me
The sound of cicadas pats my heart for a long time

163. The existence of fate(운명의 존재)

Fate that a single hair shakes the body

No matter how hard you try, you can't help it

Coming suffering refers to the existence of fate

Sit on your eyebrows and cross their arms, whoops

If you give enough to throw your life

You can change your destiny but

You have to follow the trend of the times

The meaning was set early

Drugs can't cure the disease

Disease can't take a person

Grow your energy by controlling yin and yang

Sometimes starving finds a way to survive

You say you'd rather eat than die of hunger

Moving the graveyard believing in fengshui and divination

You will find comfort in finding the god you serve

It's a pity that you become a puppet of fate

It's too late to know it's going the way you built it

164. A mind to keep dust free(티 없는 배려심)

When you turn on the air conditioner,
the ghostly dust dances before the cold wind blows
The white dust of a tissue that has been pulled out
covers the earth like volcanic ash
They wipe their mouths as if they knew nothing

The boss who ate first at the staff cafeteria
He dusts off his top and wears it
Tear off a lot of toilet paper, wipes the little water off,
and then throws it away
Don't waste it because it's not yours, in addition
I'm more concerned about the occurrence of dust

When you gracefully shake your long hair in the car
Fluttering stupid dust will pull out the pillar roots
of anyone's chest at any time

You may have seen turtles die from plastic
If the tiny particles emitted by the chemical fibers
get stuck in the body, they can cause fatal injuries

Keep away from the kid who swishes his socks off

in front of your nose, even if he's handsome

It's quite obvious as if looking a dust!

On Global Warming, nature's providence

Don't just give lip service to environmental issues

With the right mind so that there's no dust

Fundamental consideration is the key to the environment

Dusting out of the duvet dangerously by the high window

165. Pi's Teachings(파이의 가르침)

Know the circumference of a circle by diameter times Pi?
Not a delicious pumpkin pie
The answer to the thought is that Pi is outer space

With what ruler do you measure the curved line
Run around with my feet instead of my head
I found that perfect circle Pi

Even if your mouth is dry as you run
The saliva that comes out of running one more round

In the digestive power of chewing forty-eight times
Rolling saliva and nosebleeds prevent cavities
Swallowing saliva can prevent diabetes

Any ailment inside the body can be cured by starvation
The skin is repaired by applying soil or licking it
These are traditional healing methods

Top Secrets of the Unsolved Pi know yourself
The three beat energy of difficulty buried in the rough
The pi of reincarnation that will be buried in the end
In the teaching of looking into one's body and mind
I'm trying hard to get rid of the mysterious dawn

166. I run(달리기)

Alone on the playground where the smile of the moon rolls

Warm up and breathe slowly running

The shadows of trees on the border entangled in streetlights,

creating graduation caps, crosses, and diamonds

Sometimes the morning star whispers to me

When the sweat on my forehead wets my chest

The mutant delusion that rises with the sound of breathing

disappears following the footsteps

A piece of sweet wind passes like a watermelon

In the garden where the sun is stretching and rubbing his eyes,

the sound of sparrows biting on jewels is noisy

Even if it becomes difficult to breathe after running a few laps

Running is a medicine for unstable knee pain

After do 10 chin ups, becomes stiff and the workout is over

Thinking of the next person, put the garbage in one place

The confidence of a refreshing morning exercise makes me run

the Olympics of Son Ki-jung and Nam Seung-ryong

167. Beyond oblivion(망각을 넘어서)

If you forget, you can leave
Just alone

If you forget your hometown,
you'll wander around without feeling unfamiliar
If you forget love
you don't have to fall attachment
If you forget life
no fear of dying
If you forget your memory
others don't know
You can go your own way

Drug treatment is not reasonable
Who would have a warm hand?

Splash splash, The wandering oblivion
brings the clouds and knocks on my head
Even in the shower that wets whole body
the grass-blade stands pure and truthful

Okay

Let's go beyond oblivion

* Learn how to treat dementia with 3 exercises
  Dynamic movement -Tightrope walking
  Movement in the quiet -Chant Sutras
  Static motion -Meditation

168. A desire to benefit oneself(비기지욕)

Don't let your heart down or try to empty it
There is no dustpan, and it might get on my feet

What could be more delicious and more enjoyable
In a world that has looked all over with boundless greed
No matter how much I have to fill it up,
No message will come

Take it all, there will be a space you can set your heart
So I will fill it up, so you diligently empty it
Does it need to be empty to float or fill up to fly
the silent spaceship

When I breathe quietly, all kinds of delusions flutter
Anguish wanders from death to life
It becomes a question mark that falls down
like a dragonfly on the glabella

Don't try to empty the heart that can't be empty

When the desire to empty is filled with fog

What to do

In the wretched greed

Nirvana that empties even emptiness

Saying that living is practice asceticism

The mother river

Ganges flows

169. Sparrows are flying(참새 날다)

When the eastern sky sprouts with clear energy
Pull your feet in a comfortable breathing position
Bring a nice shadow in the phantasmagoria
A flower that blooms humbly with elaborate thoughts

On the sweet Roman Holiday
Even farewell is fresh love
The love that can transcend

Tilt tilt your head
But
The bright sparrows sitting on the ridge tile
know the taste of soaring up in no time

Every morning like this
Proudly fill your empty chest with the right energy
Fly without hesitation
Flap fluttering into the Forest of Achievement

170. The decimal system(십진법)

"Grandpa, would you like some oranges?"
"Yeah, just(one) bring two three or four."
Grandson brought ten
"Too many."
"In all, there are ten."
Yo cute boy!

"Forward march!"
"One

Two

Three

Four

One two three four, one two three four."

East West North and South in one round
Become ten and open
When I collect only four, it becomes ten

As the sun shines through the dark clouds
I perceived it a long time later

171. In front of white porcelain(백자 앞에서)

The ecstasy of the frugal and innocent white coat
The figure of white porcelain, a symbol of traditional beauty
Goryeo inlay celadon of the world's best blue color
It's a real luxury that transcends time and space

Beyond the curtain that I approached quietly
Fighting spirit permeated pitifully
I think stones will fly from anywhere at any moment
Pride that is secretly admired with care

The impatience buried in antiques, ceramics
and jittery glassware seeps into itself
A place where people's hearts are divided by worries

Fortunately, neither the affection nor the village were
scattered into several pieces
Sotheby's auction house's breathtaking discernment

With faith that does not crack even if it is small

In the frame of solid affection of iron culture

Turn anxiety into relief and positive thoughts

May the value of life continue comfortably

The scared breath that might spill or shatter

With the weight that touches the white teacup

The taste to savor is astringent

172. Cutting water with a knife(칼로 물 베기)

If you keep fighting with your wife over again

saying that you are cutting water with a knife

You'll stamp your divorce papers

Let's split the water in the washbasin

It leaves a mark on a whole vessel

Water opens its blue eyes and stares

Don't swing it clumsily because it's easy

Water remembers everything

Will water in a plate just harm people?

Haha, look at that water with the mirror

It's holding a twinkling sword

It grasp the situation like lightning

Many know that supreme right is like water, but

If you can't run like a sharpened knife

Words and water are all useless

After using a knife to save a person

Finish with clear water

Can water hold a dagger in its chest

173. Smoking booth(흡연 부스)

On a street full of yellow dust, Fight fire with fire
In the smoking booth,
where men and women of all ages are mixed up
Thick smoke blooms free from all thoughts and ideas

To neglect the pleasures of others
Etiquette and health are befogged
A lukewarm spring day burns and
disappears like an azalea

Despite the promises with children and
the warnings of harsh advertisements
Tolerating the unbearable is always short-lived
There is no difference in the resolution of three days

To an isolated space built as if pushed away
It becomes a zoo of spectacles that you stare at
There is no way to heal the dry heart of agony
In a city of suffocating chaos

In Schindler's List's Gas Chamber of Solitude
The history of an innocent cry is passing by

174. White hair praise(백발 예찬)

White hair that doesn't care about youth
Rather than dyeing it black and looking old
don't you look so healthy

Even if there are gentlemen who yield quickly
Don't askance your eyes on the place of a weak child
With that fresh heart of being still young
Making a pregnant woman sit makes you feel good

If you don't have a car, scold the foolish National Assembly
You can easily overcome the barrier of wisdom
Even if a body that stands upright is burdensome and difficult

Can you say that you know death without dying
Beyond the white-haired New Year that approaches like flames
If I run ahead, hope will spring up

Even in the old morning when the razor bites the flesh
The bitter heart leaves the years far away
Winter is grinning at white hair in the mirror

If the base of the head is dark and pretty in my opinion

escorting the old road of those who ride on a palanquin

in Jokduri(bride's headpiece)

I want to ride a white horse despite my gray hair

The days when the farming goes well and everyone enjoys rest

Gently straighten last year's troubled hair

Fly neatly with the adoring white hair

175. On a rainy day(비 오는 날)

The nostalgic rain is pouring

The relationship that disappeared like a shooting star

If it scatters with raindrops

The islands of the sea that sit apart

Everyone gets wet alone

On the earth where memories tickle

The misty solitude of the spray shines faintly

Water cleaning on a rainy day

A bitterly smeared piece of black memory

Remove stains that are probably 100 years old

Still, the accumulated regrets

Pour it into the plaintiveness

infinitely in an empty heart

I miss the rain that I miss

Without an umbrella

Rhododendron wet in the rain

miss you, even if get limp from longing

love that you know but you don't know it

Putting aside the stinging of pine needles

all the way through spring

I suffer from longing in the rain

176. Fastidious personality(별난 성격)

"Bushik." The stone that I chewed while eating

"Dirty!" This hair in the soup

Even plastic shavings jumped in

Coffee tastes bad

How can this only happen to me

They say it's because I have a weird temper

Even though I tried to be good

Because of the blind ghosts

Your heart surrounded by sighs

I heard the sound of "click" while eating shellfish

I spit it out and there's a pearl in it

It hurts with a funny and painful mouth covered

A precious looking pearl is hidden in a drawer

My anger fades into my wife's skirt

It seeps in and disappears like white dust

177. In the snowy forest(눈 오는 숲속)

It's snowing
Filter out the white rumors
It pours piece by piece

Stories of how hard they endured
by bumping into each branch
Hiding a fiery smile and hovering

Even if the sound of white breath is bruised
While dancing around the world
Permeates with traces of truth

A narrow path chasing memories
In the shady forest
Through unfulfilled sorrows
In the tears that are wet without knowing
Fluttering through the old days

It's snowing

Even if I feel sorry for the world

I wish white snow would fall

for five hundred years

Lay with outstretched arms on the cozy snow

Pull the white dream hanging on the branch

In the forest

that gently covers the fault of anger

Innocent cry is in full bloom

178. Tick Tock(째깍째깍)

Fighting for seconds to get ahead of time
Rolex and Omega on the treadwheel
Between waving each other's handsome arms
Enduring the short time more hastily

A short time runs well hurry-scurry
A long time goes by slowly in a dither

If you want to go fast, go alone
The long road goes together
Sadness that becomes someone's joy
The joy of being someone's sorrow
In a fierce competition

A painful moment passing by holding
the neck of the rough hourglass
Forgetting to let death take care of itself
Frequently cross the hands of a clock of fate

In a different perspective of the flow that we took off

The miracle is to change your mind

The ripples that were struggling are realized

From a different perspective of Flow we threw away

A miracle is to change your mind

Realize and know the ripples you've been through

Secretly wanting to get ahead of the times,

Tick tock, tick tock, the incited nidana with scramble

Even bright steps are chased away

Can't help but burn to adore the fantasy

179. Obstacle and Stepping Stone
(걸림돌 디딤돌)

Parents pray that they do not disturb their children

Their sons cry that their parents are not stepping stones

Because the medicine of the gap has a different taste

A crossroads selection in the search for wisdom

On the stone beak that made me stumble seven times

Stepping stones that are easily erected eight times

That it is a rock touched by the influence of the heart

If you cut the stumbling block and turn it into a stepping stone,

As if climbing the floor with happy steps

Get rid of the blocked barbed wire entanglement quickly

Let the country bloom with beautiful flowers

In the abyss that left scars in my heart

Stepping on a stepping stone that can afford learning

Many obstacles became stepping stones

Holding on to all the obstacles in this world

As if supporting and raising it with an A-frame carrier pole

My teacher, who turns them into stepping stones,

Trims the flower buds in a friendly embrace

180. Search word(검색어)

I typed it into the search bar on my computer
how much I don't know
In the deep meaning of an old saying like a jewel
I wonder if this word will be used

The excellent medical acupuncture of the East
revealed in the emperor's inner sutras
Korean Hanja recognized by Joo Eun-rae and Imeo-dang
We're the only ones in a culture that says it's not ours
A country that made a fuss saying it was unnecessary
Can we proudly stop the Northeast Project?

It originates from an unusually weak sense of inferiority,
We are divided by a clash of group interests
A widespread shambles of arrogance, hypocrisy, and lies

When the chronic inflammation that exists inside spreads
In the search for future prediction,
Instead of unification, it ignited into a world war
It will be a beautiful country that will disappear into ashes

I forgot what I was trying to find on the screen
Heaven and earth contained in the far-fading sky
A new world engulfed in flames
How do I say this word that's not even in the search?

181. The sky, the earth, and the flowers
(하늘과 땅과 꽃)

The red petals bloom with passion
The yellow petals bloom innocently
One heart on one petal
How much love has come and gone

Not to forget the covenant made between heaven and earth
The season of love that has been guarded unwaveringly

In what harmony with the black sky and yellow earth
Add fine water to the angel's wings
A variety of flowers that are more harsh on innocence

These petals proudly hold the sky
That flower stalk is firmly on the ground
In the world of flower buds where countless thoughts gather
A beautiful ten-day dream in full bloom

I wonder if there is a single petal without a story

Without opening all the inner feelings that it has kept

In the brief meeting before the tears dry

The hot blooming flower makes me sick

The flexible true light embroidered in the void

Where I persuaded the snow-covered fields

A flower that absorbs the sesame-like universe

182. Flesh-colored crayons(살색 크레용)

He told me to paint it black later
First on the face of a running child
I painted the flesh tint nicely

The sports day picture drawn with crayon stubs
The picture, which won the special prize, sat at the
top of the bulletin board and shone with surprise

Pink petals fluttering in the wind
A flower boat on the river, waving the hand
I look back at my suffocating appearance

On a spring day after eleven years plus sixty
Faces painted in flesh color are lovely
I breathe deeply when I see a smile without eyes

Even if I draw and draw again, the faces I miss
When pressed with pain that cannot be drawn
With the lonely pine needles that split the wind
The flames in the furnace is a swell dance

Even if the face I just drew turns black

Pulling the arrow that fades like that

I'm holding the flesh color again on the drawing paper

Suddenly the name was changed to Apricot

I look at what color the sky is

183. Still looking for foreign goods
(난 아직 외제를 찾는다)

Chocolate given by an American soldier was so sweet

When it comes to Japanese products,

there were times when we might be crazy about it

Different perceptions of quality for export and domestic consumption

A chunk of meat that claims ours is good

We're constantly looking for imported kimchi while ignoring it

It's our painful belief that we haven't reached yet

In the myriad of goods waiting for the owner

I'm curious to see if there's anything useful

Excellent daily necessities from a country with a long history

A luxury item that will last for many years if you buy it once

Even if these are unavoidable

High happiness index in Bhutan or Finland

Danish Integrity, Japanese Kindness

Bring these good things meaningfully

I wish we could put it on our cell phone

There are many things that even rich countries do not have

There are many good examples even in difficult countries

Pick and remove the bad ones

Find the overflowing humanity somewhere

Rolling my mouse here and there on the earth

184. The Gate(문)

I coughed through the open door
The door puts twin wicks on its eyes and asks
Said that the thief made the door of the heart shut
The door through which money enters and exits is open

The future is closed to the fuss of the past
The open door is filled with arrogance and hatred
The door of hypocrisy that rejects the other side
The gates of hell that fell into the abyss sinkhole

Hang a noose on the dark door
Don't make the night of a person who walks the night cry

I said 'open the door' to the iron gate
The door that gently opens as if to welcome longing
The door of a warm heart that was tightly closed

A door that is not biased with a sturdy door frame
I want to be happy like this, the guilty blessing
A door that could be opened in 500 years
Thousands of years are the flowers of the door of truth

I'm afraid I'll open the open door and close the closed door
'Open sesame'
I dare to shout the truth that will be buried

185. Kid and eraser(아이와 지우개)

A kid drawing with pencil in sketchbook
In a palace-like house with a large yard
Grandpa, grandma, dad and mom
He also draws his brother's sharp nose

To redraw crooked pants
he erase the picture with the eraser
It looks like there are a lot of people,
so he erase his grandparents
Parents look at the picture over his shoulders

Only black marks remain and cannot be forgotten
Darkness will bring dawn
Even when the sun rises,
there are things that never rise again
The child does not know yet

As the kid drew the pants straight and cool,
Parents stroking the child's head with loving hands
Dad smiles at mom and
The child is holding an eraser

186. Mt. Geumgang(금강산)

What is this? It's clothes. Come in.
What is that? It's pine nuts. Please eat.
What is this? It's K-traditional hat. Go away.

Kim Sat-gat, who dared freeload and went on a tour
Had he mastered the sermon of The Golden Sutra
with 12 thousand disciples

Gwimyeonam, the mourning face of Prince Maui,
Why are Guryong Falls and Maitreya Buddha
still washing clean water with the wind?

In the idea of rocks and water that quietly permeates
In the years that unfold like falling pine cones
I toss and turn my head lest my fingers miss the moon

Mount Gaegol where dreams are lost and

the stars are shooting without mercy

Beautiful Pungak and Bongrae which has stopped blooming

Through the shrunken shadows from jealous of harmony

A handful of pure rain and wind longs to wake up

Where are you from and where are you going

I asked the way to get to Birobong

It is said to follow the breath while breathing blue

Samseonam unconsciously scatters sunlight

187. Meditation on the Border(경계에 선 명상)

In front of the bright window, there's me standing on the border

When I open the window, there's only a difference in eyelids

Neither man nor himself nor faith nor money nor staff

At the sad limit of getting hurt when broken

A plaintive wind quivers the paper weather strip

Throwing away the will and emptiness, it touches me as if hesitating

At the crossroads of opening and closing, coming and going,

taking and throwing away, sickness and healing

Is it just the pathetic memories of passing by?

Struggled me so much while alive

Did death become longing because it cried so much

The tears that spread while laughing are full

The laughter that sheds while crying is just far away

Couldn't even plant a single trust between meeting and parting

Walking on a path that is neither a movie

nor a three act nor a cloud

The weeping willows pulled their arms and stretched out hotly

They don't want to run after the river,

the water that revolves around the stream

In the trap of fear of not knowing what to lose

thinking of death as the best way out

Green shouts overflowing on the shimmering border

188. Dog poop for medicine(약에 쓰는 개똥)

I said it's dog poop

It vanished without a trace, you just stare at my lips

Is medicine the only thing you don't have when you need it

A wise man tells me to look at the moon, not his finger

'Cause I don't even know what staring moon is

Arguing right and wrong about the finger

Even if you want to keep the moon and poop away

To the awakening beyond the sudden attraction

Would you like to touch your mind once

Who do you think you are (What is wisdom?)

The moon carrying dog poop

Rise high free from bondage

그리움 한 두레박

1판 1쇄 발행 2023년 01월 17일

지은이 남백현

교정 신선미 편집 이혜리
마케팅 박가영 총괄 신선미

펴낸곳 (주)하움출판사 펴낸이 문현광

이메일 haum1000@naver.com 홈페이지 haum.kr
블로그 blog.naver.com/haum1007 인스타 @haum1007

ISBN 979-11-6440-299-1(03800)

좋은 책을 만들겠습니다.
하움출판사는 독자 여러분의 의견에 항상 귀 기울이고 있습니다.